DARK

VI CARTER

WARNING

This book is a dark romance. This book contains scenes that may be triggering to some readers and should be read by those only 18 or older.

NEWSLETTER

JOIN MY NEWSLETTER AND NEVER MISS A NEW RELEASE OR GIVEAWAY

*Scan the QR Code
to be taken to my
newsletter page.*

CHAPTER ONE

"**D**ance for me."

A soft melody plays in the background, its beat is designed for swaying hips. I want to open my eyes, but the earlier warning to keep them closed has my lashes resting on my cheeks. Wringing my hands behind my back I squeeze my eyes tighter. The crop top I wear just barely covers my breasts, doing very little to hide the humiliation that burns my chest. I keep my hands firmly joined so I don't start yanking at the top.

"Don't fidget. Do as you're told and most importantly keep your eyes closed at all times." Linda's words of warning were given before we entered the room.

So, I am doing as I am told and not fidgeting. My black stilettos click on the oak polished floor as I move slowly from one foot to the other. My face burns as Linda sniggers at my stiff and mechanical movements. Anger races through me and I'm tempted to open my eyes, but I don't. Her warning to me was clear. I'm not allowed to set my eyes on my new master. I'm not worthy, she had told me the first day I had arrived here. I wanted to tell her that I didn't want to be worthy. The only thing I wanted was to go home. Not be here in this castle with this man that my father had sold me to. I've been here three weeks and the pain of being sold by my own father to clear his gambling debt still pierces me.

"Is that how you dance for me?" A shiver races across my bare arms and I stop dead in my tracks. His voice is behind me. Every fiber of my being is awake, alert. I want to turn and see the man who bought me. His breath touches my bare back. His question is filled with disappointment.

Letting out a heavy breath that shakes on the end, I listen to the music again and find the beat. Dipping my head, I let it fill me as my hips move to the music. I don't think of how I've been sold or how humiliating this is. My eyes burn and I pour all that anger into the dance. My hips sway wider, my head rises.

"Good girl." His breath brushes my cheek. The heat of his body is right behind me. I falter slightly but find my rhythm again. I hate his praise. I hate him. I hate my father. I move faster finding the freedom I am seeking in the music. My hands flutter out to either side of me, controlling the movement of my hips as the music picks up its pace, crossing that mountain that I'm racing across with the tempo. Throwing my head back, I allow myself to smile as I move my body as if a lover's hands were caressing me. Linda no longer sniggers and no one else interrupts my dance. I'm not sure if he is still behind me, but I continue to move until the song ends and I'm left standing in the silent room, feeling a bit breathless. The silence has me searching behind my eyelids for a change in the darkness that I have become accustomed to.

"Were you a dancer before?" His voice is no longer behind me.

His question catches me off guard. "What?" I shuffle, moving to try and follow the flow of his deep, hard voice.

"Answer him." Linda's voice pierces the silence. She always sounds like she is one moment away from exploding. Like every button of hers has been pressed one too many times.

"No." I hold my breath and stand rigid like a circus monkey waiting to hear what my next trick will be. No one speaks and the longer I stand here half-naked, the more fear seems to grow in me. I've waited for the last three weeks to be raped or tortured, but instead, I'm made to dance for this man. I don't think anyone else is ever in the room, aside from Linda. I have no idea what she is to him. A lover? Possibly. I have no idea why I'm not allowed to see him. Is he scarred or deformed? My eyes continue to search the darkness. I am sure I'm the only other person here; I've never heard—or seen—anyone else.

The castle that I've been brought to is one I've visited several times. I just had no idea that anyone lived here. It's open to the public all year 'round. A select amount of rooms showcase what it would have looked like in its glory days. The part I'm in is far more modern. But you didn't doubt that you were in a grand castle.

A small, warm hand touches my bare arm and I'm escorted from the room. I turn my head in the direction his voice always comes from, but I don't dare open my eyes. I think he's tall, his voice is deep, but I have no idea of the rest.

The click of the door behind me acts as a signal, telling me it's finally safe to look up. The light hurts my eyes for a moment. Linda moves me forward. Her sharp features are striking, high cheekbones, and a perfectly straight nose. Thin lips that never smile. She's every photographer's dream, that is if you get past the darkness in her brown eyes. She carries it like a shield.

Red nails wrap around my forearm and squeeze slightly when I don't walk quickly enough. She never speaks to me like a person, and after the first few days here, I gave up.

We reach my room and that is where Linda takes her leave. Blonde hair cut close to her head doesn't take away from her hard beauty as she gives me one final look. The door closes in my face and I hate the silence immediately.

Turning, I catch myself in the full-length mirror. I look cheap. My eyes burn again and I push down the pain as I kick off the stilettos. Shimmying out of the black skirt, I walk straight to the wardrobe and get out the only thing that isn't degrading, a white silk nightgown. Putting it on, it falls just above my knees, covering my half-naked body.

Several thoughts race through my mind like they do every day. Why did my father sell me? I know he has a large debt to this man, but who sold their only child, their only daughter to someone? What does this man want with me? So far I've been clothed, fed, and given a room. But I know this won't last forever. Double doors are wide open as I walk into my bathroom. It's half the size of my room here, which is also a ridiculous size. I spend most of my days trapped in here pretending that I live here and I can leave my room whenever I want. I just don't want to. Tying my hair up, silky black strands manage to escape the tie and dangle around my face. I push them back as I face the mirror. Frightened green eyes stare back at me, sparkling with uncertainty. I look away unable to face what I see reflected back at me. The white hand basin holds me up as I grip either side of it. Memories of my life slip through my hands like sand as my chest tightens. It feels as if someone has sucked all the air from the room and I lose my grip. The walls close in as I hit the tiled floor hard. The ceiling hovers over me a million light-years away. Gold coving dips and melts as my brain short circuits.

Blue eyes, like the blue of the clearest sky, stare down at me. The softness of the bed under me molds around my back. I can't look away. His eyes are kind and not what I expected. He isn't scarred, his tanned skin is smooth, he looks normal. My gaze flickers around the room as I look for Linda, but she isn't here. Fear skitters across my skin, dampening it in its wake. We've never been alone before. I've wondered for three weeks what this man looks like. Now that I'm face to face with him, all I wanted to do is close my eyes and *un-see* him. I fear the consequences.

"Do you know what happened?"

His voice is wrong. It's too high pitched, too gentle. I was so used to that raspy, deep, hard voice. This isn't him. I try to sit up, but my head swims.

"You need to rest." Gentle hands push me back down. "You've hit your head pretty hard." His words send a sharp pain to my head. I remember looking in the mirror and then I couldn't breathe.

"I couldn't breathe," I whisper.

"You will be okay."

My focus is back on his blue eyes. The silver scope around his neck comes into view. I hadn't noticed it before.

"You're a doctor?" I say trying to sit up again. Instead of making me stay still, he helps me sit up, fixing several pillows behind me.

"Yes, I am. I can assure you, you will be fine." His soft smile has my stomach twisting. I stare at him until his smile slowly disappears. My heart beats rapidly as my mind screams to beg him to get me out of here. I swallow. If I left, my father would be killed. That's the deal. He deserves to die. He really does, but I'm not about to sign my own father's death sentence. I break eye contact with the doctor and will my heart to slow down.

The door to my bedroom opens and Linda walks in. She captivates the doctor. Her hips sway perfectly in her black and white pencil skirt. The white shirt is see-through, her black bra on full display.

"Doctor Rodgers, how is our patient?" Linda's lips do something I have never seen them do before; they lift into a half smile. She looks slightly innocent—or is youthful more accurate? She no longer has that tortured look she normally wears.

"She's doing fine. A bit more rest and she will be right as rain." His blue eyes flicker to me, it's brief like I'm the last thing he wants to talk about. His focus is now back on Linda.

"You're a lifesaver." Linda stops at my bedside and looks down at me like I mean something to her. "She gave us all quite the scare."

Was there a threat in her words? I wasn't sure. I sink further into the pillows. "Sorry. I'm not sure what happened."

She barks a short soft laugh. "One too many drinks."

"With Gerald?" Linda's smile falters at Doctor Rodgers' question.

"No." She answers quickly. "We better not keep you." She holds out his bag to him with a forced smile. My brain is spinning on the name Gerald. Is that his name?

The doctor's brows pull down at his quick dismissal. He takes the bag with uncertainty. "Are you sure you don't need me to stay and keep an eye on her?"

"We have already taken up enough of your time." Linda widens her arm, a gesture for him to come along.

He does so with disappointment in his voice. "Okay. Well, you know where I am."

It hits me hard after the door closes—I'm alone again. I stare at the door, the minute's tick by and melt into one another. I want to use my voice, I want to break the silence but words are useless, they will shatter the silence only briefly before it pieces itself back together, it becomes more solid and stronger. I learn to accept what I can't change. Closing my eyes, I let the darkness in and surprisingly, I find sleep.

When I open my eyes the room is dark. I don't have windows in my room. My eyes skitter across the darkness. Someone turned off my lights, they were always left on. I push back the blanket and step out onto the cold wooden floor, the coldness absorbs some of the heat that pulses through me. I close my eyes and listen. I can hear his breath. I know he's here. My eyes roam across the room and I'm sure the space across from my bed is darker, deeper.

I step towards the darkness. My knees wobble a little.

"Dance for me." My heart skips a beat at the sound of his voice. I'm prodding the darkness trying to make out his features, but the darkness molds around him like he's part of it. He's here in my room. This is something that has never happened before. I know I should be terrified, but a large part of me wants to see him, or ask him if his name really is Gerald. But I don't have the courage.

"I don't have music." My voice wobbles and I take another step towards him and then pause. My pulse spikes as I wait for his response, but it doesn't come. The shadows don't move so I know he is still here, waiting for me to dance. If I don't, will he step closer? Will he demand me to dance, or will he just leave?

Closing my eyes, my heart beats wildly in my ears and I take a calming breath before I start to move. Swaying my hips, I don't move closer to him but dance to my own music in front of him. I keep my eyes closed as I move slowly. I don't allow myself to acknowledge the fact that I like dancing for him. Or that he makes me feel something I have never felt before. I stop dancing and open my eyes. Disgust at my own thoughts has me wrapping my arms tightly around my waist. My eyes seek him in the darkness, but he's not there. Closing my eyes I seek out his breathing, but I can't hear it. He's gone.

Moving quickly I flick on the lights. Facing the wall my heart pounds as I slowly turn around. The thought of seeing his face has my pulse throbbing in my neck.

My room is empty. He's gone.

CHAPTER TWO

HIM

Her hips sway and I'm mesmerized by the rhythm of her body. I want to mold her with my hands, but it's too soon. *Not much longer*, I tell myself. The need to have her has me shifting in my seat. I could take her right now if I wanted to, even with Linda in the room. Linda wouldn't care, it was only skin after all. She's seen far worse things. I refocus on Cara. Right now she's lost in the moment. She has no idea how sultry she is. Her body demands my attention, and she has it. The brandy beside me sits untouched. Her arms flutter out from either side of her and I can see her on a stage commanding a room full of men. She was made for the spotlight. It's nearly a sin to keep her to myself. Each curve moves to entice, she has no idea what she is doing to me. She slowly stops as the music dies, the smile slipping from her face. The frightened little girl is back now. She's aware of everything about herself. How she stands, and the way she holds her arms. Her discomfort sends a thrill through me, I want her more now. She's prey. But it's all too easy. If I take her now, I will never stop taking, with or without her permission. Her eyes move rapidly behind her lids and I need to distract myself before I take her, right here and now.

"Were you a dancer before?" I ask, already knowing she wasn't. She was a wallflower, always has been.

"What?" she sounds so bewildered as she shuffles from one foot to another.

I can sense Linda's irritation. "Answer him." She barks and I glance at her. She's staring at Cara, hoping she steps out of line. But Linda knows that this is different. Cara isn't one of the girls that *need* to be controlled. Cara needs to lose control so I can rein her back in.

"No." Her breathy answer has me shifting in my seat again. Her chest rises and falls now as she stands bewildered. Her chest is being revealed inch by inch as her top rises slightly. Linda selected her clothes, and they were perfect. Not too much skin was showing, but enough for my mind to trace each curve and fill in the blanks. My endurance is slipping. A nod towards Linda has her standing up and taking Cara from the room.

The brandy hits the back of my throat as I drink the full glass down. Rolling the cigar in my hand I'm picturing Cara, with her curves and pouty mouth. All the things I could make her do.

"We have another one for you," Linda speaks from the door and I glance at her.

"Has he potential?" I question, hoping he doesn't. I need a release and I'll find it this way instead.

"I didn't talk to him personally."

Standing, I remove the tie from around my neck before making my way to the basement. There are two ways to reach the basement, one way is from my kitchen, the second is outside near the outhouses that act as our club. It's private, and members know they can relax and enjoy the finer things in life. My living quarters are situated at the back of the castle. No one is prohibited to enter. I give the visitors what they want as long as my own space is left alone, and it is. Moving through the sterile gray kitchen, I open a small door that leads down into the basement.

A young man in gray slacks and a gray jacket lounges on the red rose chair. He's relaxed and looks like he's waiting for a doctor's appointment.

"Do you know who I am?" I question straight away before he can see me.

"Lady Linda's muscle?" His voice is young, and glancing at him now while rolling up my sleeves confirms it.

"Look, there really is no problem; whatever it costs I can pay for it." The cockiness of his words makes me grin.

I glance at Damien who stands directly behind the boy. "Did you hear that Damien? He can pay." Damien sniggers and the boy's skin pales further, maybe he is starting to understand that this isn't a doctor's appointment.

"You can go," I tell Damien who leaves with a smirk on his face. Damien is the muscle in the club. Anyone causing problems is removed quietly and brought here, to me.

"Did your daddy never tell you that money doesn't fix everything?" I ask standing directly in front of him. That isn't true. Money fixes everything for me.

He shifts in his seat. "Look, man, I know you got your orders, but I'm sure if I could speak to Lady Linda, I could straighten this whole thing out."

I grin again. "You have two choices. I can either keep you or kill you. That's it." That's the motto I live by. Anyone who crosses me either joins me, or I kill them. No one walks away from me or pays their way out of trouble. I've made one exception to this rule, and that was Cara's father. I allowed him to pay his way out of debt—with his daughter. When I offered him the option, I didn't think he would actually accept it. When he did, I wasn't sure if I wanted to kill him or hug him. Anyone coming to this establishment knows it's a zero- tolerance facility. Our customers are selected carefully, but not carefully enough. Money isn't enough to get in here. I need to straighten that out and this boy will become an example.

He tuts and stands up out of his chair. "Look man, just get me Linda." I love this part. They have no notion of who I really am. Letting Linda be the lady of the manor—or in this case the castle—allows me to do what I really enjoy doing. Breaking things. It's what I do best.

My hands collide with his chest, forcing him into the chair. "Linda isn't coming. It's me and you; that's it. So this is your choice?" I remove my hand and he stands up. "Keep or kill."

His eyes shoot around the room. "Are you serious?" He sounds unsure. "You do know who my dad is?" His confusion in this situation is growing and so is my frustration.

"I don't care who your daddy is, but I'm sure if you went to one of his businesses and hurt a member of his staff he wouldn't be happy."

"She's a dancer, she's replaceable." His words are filled with the same cockiness that he displayed earlier.

"I'm going to make the executive decision…" I pause and he relaxes further into his chair like we are on the same page, and that one of my dancers is replaceable. "I've decided to kill you." My hand easily circles the back of his neck as I drag him out of the chair and release him onto his knees on the concrete floor.

"What the fuck!" My knee connects with his mouth cutting off his words. Blood spills and my own blood starts to pump. There is always that moment I want them to fight back, but they never do.

My foot connects with his stomach, he spins and lands on the broad of his back, gasping for air. Grabbing his overpriced jacket, I drag him from the floor and make him stand. The crunch is satisfactory as his nose crunches against my fist. "She was our best dancer," I tell him before slamming my fist into his face again. Blood splashes my white shirt.

"Now look what you did." I point at my stained shirt.

Blood pours from his lips as he starts to beg. "I'm sorry."

His stomach curls around my knee as I slam into him with full force before dropping him to the ground. As he fights for air, I get my gun from the small box that sits inside the only cabinet in the room. This gun has been used more times than I care to admit. Taking it off safety, I point it at the boy. "Get up."

He glances up at me as fear widens his half-sunken eyes. He rises using one arm, the other hanging loosely by his side. "Keep. Keep." He shouts the word at me like a lifeline and unfortunately it is. One I try to ignore as I point the gun at his head.

"Please man, I'll do anything. Just don't kill me." He cries while shuffling on the spot.

I lower the gun. "What's your name?"

He looks around the room disorientated and bewildered. "Mickey."

"Mickey, your decision has been noted. I'll be in touch." I turn my back on him and put my gun back. No doubt I'll get to use it soon. There's always a clown to be shot.

"That's it?" He shrugs.

"Why are you still here?" I ask. Normally they would have run from the room.

"It seems too easy."

I grin. "Nothing about this is easy. I'll be in touch."

I leave the basement first and make my way back to my living quarters. Returning to my library, I close the door behind me and open the laptop to check in on Cara. She's asleep. A soft knock on my door has me closing the laptop.

"We've had a busy hour since you left." Linda steps in and I push away from my desk. Her eyes glance over the blood spots on my shirt before she continues. "Cara collapsed."

I stop unbuttoning my shirt.

"She's fine. Doctor Rodgers checked her over, and she's fine."

I nod at Linda and finish removing my shirt.

"Her father was also here again."

My temper flares. *Stupid man.* He just can't accept the deal he made. "I hope you sent him packing," I say to Linda.

"I think killing him would be the best." Linda doesn't blink and I know her decision isn't emotional, it's from a very controlled place. But still, I don't like it.

"No. He's not to be touched." I finish taking off my shirt and throwing it in the trash can. "Has he been escorted home?"

Picking up my phone, I switch over to the camera. Cara's sleeping face fills the small screen.

"Yes. He wants her back. He threatened to go to the Gardaí, maybe you should give her back."

I look up at Linda now. "No." I leave the room. Handing Cara back isn't an option.

Once I have a clean white shirt on, I lay my phone down and do something I haven't done before. She's still asleep when I enter her room. Turning off the lights I stand across from her bed and watch the rise and fall of her chest. My eyes adjust quickly to the dark and she stirs, something in me stirs too. I've never been so brave to enter her room, being this close to her is sending waves of excitement through me. She sits up and her breathing is heavy. She's afraid. It's like she's staring at me now as she pushes back her quilt. I don't move as she steps out of the bed. I devour her as she takes an unsure step towards me, her legs wobble and she stops only a few spaces away. She's so close and I want to take her, the beast in me wants her now, with or without her permission. I still the noise inside me.

"Dance for me," I tell her.

She takes in a sharp breath as she continues to stare at me, but I don't think she can see me.

"I don't have any music." She wrings her hands together like she does when she's nervous. It takes her a moment, but she starts to move.

Good girl.

She has no idea how good she is. She's a goddess that I own. I watch for only a few more moments before I slip from her room as she continues to dance for me.

Cara, my dancer. As I close her door gently I turn, Linda's eyes meet mine and I can see the question in them, but I don't owe her an explanation.

"We have a problem." Words that are spoken here nearly daily leave Linda's lips.

CHAPTER THREE

HER

The minute my door opens the next morning, I stand. I hate the desperation that fills my limbs. I hate silence. I hate empty spaces. I'm starting to hate those brown muddy eyes that stare at me now. The red skirt and red shirt fit Linda perfectly. She closes the door behind her and I shiver when her lip raises slightly.

"You got a job." Her eyes narrow as she waits for me to speak and when I don't, she steps deeper into my room with her hands behind her back.

"So in an hour, you'll have help to get ready."

My heart slowly starts to race. "Get ready for what?" My words come out through gritted teeth. Linda's smile is slow, but it's enough to make me dread the answer.

"Master was very impressed with how you danced. So, one of his dancers is sick, and you will take her place."

Blood rushes to my head and I take a step back and sit on the bed. "A dancer? What kind of dancer?" I knew it wasn't ballet or Irish Dancing. "Linda, I'm not a dancer. Please don't do this."

She exhales loudly. "The type of dancing you've done for him here." She turns on her heel ending the conversation. I don't notice she's gone until the door clicks.

Standing up, I look around the room like I might find the answers to this madness scattered across the oak floor. Me, a dancer? Tears burn my eyes before heat burns my face. I'm not a dancer. Dread pools in my stomach as I picture a pole and drunk men throwing money at me.

The handle rattles in my hand as panic has me trying to chase Linda. The door doesn't budge. "Linda." I slam my fists into the door as I call her name.

My red fists protest as I hit the door again for what feels like the hundredth time. I'm more surprised when it opens. A large woman carrying a bag bustles in. She doesn't speak as she gives me a split second glance before placing the bag on the bed.

I'm staring at her wide back when she turns. "You want to sit down so I can start your makeup?" There is an air of annoyance to her words.

"Where am I going?" I ask her and she places a hand on her large hip. "I'm just here to do you up sweetheart, I've a lot of other girls to get through, so sit down."

I walk numbly over to the dressing table and sit as she starts to do my makeup. Once it's done, she asks me if I want to see, but I decline with a shake of my head. My heart escalates every time I think about what's happening. I know staying here in the safety of these four walls wouldn't last. The only thing I can hope is that maybe it's like a group dance, anything other than a pole.

"Your clothes are on the bed." She packs up her makeup before placing a black clothing bag on the bed.

I don't wait for her to leave before I unzip it. Taking out the hanger, I stare at the black piece of material that looks like a swimsuit. A white collar is separate along with fishnet tights. Unable to believe this is all I'm meant to wear, I search through the bag—but that's it.

I'm shaking my head when Linda steps into the room. "You were supposed to be ready by now." Her heels click loudly on the floor, I focus on the noise as my heart plays a beat I've never heard before. I'm going to pass out, and honestly, I just wish I would.

"Get dressed now." Linda's words pull me back.

"I can't do this," I tell her, shaking my head.

Her eyes hold nothing. "You can and you will." Picking up the outfit, she pushes it against my chest. "So get dressed. Now."

I count twelve girls as I stand in the middle of the room. My hands aren't large enough to cover myself up. I feel so exposed, yet no one looks at me. They are all busy getting ready. Each outfit is as skimpy as the last.

"Listen up." Linda doesn't raise her voice, yet it carries across the activity that now dies down, and everyone pays attention.

"I want one hundred percent tonight. I noticed some of you got a little sloppy last night." She stares at a young girl who stares right back at her with a challenge in her eyes. They have a stare down until the young girl looks away.

"Secondly, and this shouldn't even need to be said, but no drinking on the job." This is focused towards a redhead who's wearing a red bikini with white feathers attached around the underwear.

"Even if they are bought for us?" She asks, her red shiny lips tugging up into a smirk. She pushes her bust out as she speaks.

"Even if they are bought for you. Got it, Wendy?"

Wendy nods to Linda that she gets it. A shake has entered my knees as the focus now falls on me. "This is the new girl. I'm sure you'll all give her a friendly welcome." Linda doesn't glance at me as she leaves the room. Everyone else is staring, and the way Linda said *friendly* sounded anything but *friendly*. Wendy is the first to step towards me.

"Just watch your back. These bitches will tear into you the moment you stop watching." She pouts, kicking out her hip before walking off.

A blonde with nothing covering her small chest slams her shoulder into mine as she walks past. "Watch where you're stepping." Her large blue eyes stare back at me with unwarranted hate.

"Never mind her. She hates on everyone. I'm Candy."

My mind is spinning with all this. "I'm Cara," I answer while hugging my waist.

Candy grins at me. "You don't look like you belong here." She's smiling sweetly now.

I don't belong here—in this place—with girls like Candy. Taking in Candy's bright pink swimsuit that's not very different from my black one, she looks really good in hers. Her brown hair is clipped back randomly, strands fall around her face in soft curls. Large hoop earrings and white gloves finish off her outfit.

I shrug as she waits for me to speak.

"Cara," Linda's voice is like a lifeline to a drowning man. That's what it feels like. I move quicker than I ever have. I'm hoping that Linda sees her mistake and takes me back to my room. She pulls a pair of black stilettos from behind her back. "Put them on." They bang loudly as she drops them to the floor and I slip my feet inside them. She's walking away and I follow her.

Linda commands the space as she pushes open double black doors. The music is immediate and the atmosphere changes. The darkness of the space is only lit with soft lighting that's mostly coming from a center stage where Wendy stands now. Only a handful of men are in the large space and that eases my anxiety slightly. Small round tables with red lamps on them cast shadows across the men's faces. My eyes hop from one to the other, wondering if any of these are my master—or if his name truly is Gerald.

We stop at a round leather couch. "Sit here and watch Wendy." Linda points at the couch as she glances around the club. I sit down, my legs barely holding me up. Linda leaves and I keep glancing around the room, looking at each man to see if any of them are watching me. But they are consumed by Wendy.

Once I start to watch her, it's impossible to look away. She's so good. There is no pole, just her and this stage, and yet it works. Her body moves perfectly to the beat like the music is writing itself to her movements. She moves slowly towards the floor until her back is to us. Separating her legs, she glances over her shoulder and gives the men behind me a smile. My heart beats wildly when I think that I might have to do that. Wendy's dance slowly comes to an end and the stage goes dark. My eyes refocus on the rest of the club. The other girls are either at the bar, or on small podiums that have the dreaded pole. Two large red curtains near the back are held open slightly by gold tie backs. A man in a suit stands close to them, his hands folded in front of him. His large, wide shoulders fill the space between the curtains. He watches the men mostly, his eyes skim over me. My heart continues to beat wildly the longer I sit here. Linda has done a disappearing act.

"Hi." I give the man a quick smile and look away hoping he will leave. Instead, he slides in beside me. His beige trousers and v-neck purple jumper would look better at a golf center than a club like this. I exhale before glancing at him. His kind blue eyes and graying hair settle me a bit and I guess, in his day, he must have been very handsome.

"I'm William."

I stare at his hand a moment before taking it. "Cara."

I glance around again for Linda, and when my search is unsuccessful, I return my attention to William, who hasn't taken his eyes off me.

"I'm not like that," I say keeping my voice low.

"Like what?" His question is immediate as he moves closer to me.

"Like them."

"Who?" he asks, but the smile on his face tells me he knows exactly what I'm saying. I stand only to find his fingers wrap around my wrist.

"I only wanted to buy you a drink." He nods back at the couch for me to sit, but I stay standing.

"I'm not allowed to drink on the job." I pull my hand away but he doesn't release it. "Let me go," I say hoping the panic that's rising in me isn't visible.

"Relax." He lets my hand go only to trail his fingers down my leg.

I step away from his touch and walk away from him. This isn't happening. Am I being pimped out to men? Is this more than a dance club?

I spot Candy talking to the guy in the suit. She says a few words and he nods before leaving with her. My eyes roam the room again for Linda but she isn't here. The red curtains are in front of me and I walk through. I pause at a large wooden door and hesitate. This isn't a good idea so why am I pushing down the handle and pushing the door open? A long hallway greets me. Closing the door behind me has all the noise of the club ceasing. The diamond carpet under me is lit up with red lights attached to the walls. I pass several closed doors. A black iron attachment to each acts as a small window to look inside them. None of them are open and when I reach the end of the hall, I start walking back. No one is here. A groan behind a door has me pausing. I take a step closer and listen. Grunts, someone is grunting. A male. The large oak door that I walked through seems a long way away as I stare at it. A thud from behind the door has me moving back, the grunts cease. Was someone hurt?

The small iron window has a red material behind it as I pull it open. The space isn't the size of my hand but it allows me to see into the room where the noises have been coming from. A hairy back is my first view; under him is a girl who looks ghostly white. It's her hand that dangles off the bed. I focus on it, the way it shakes with each thrust he makes inside her. The skin is too pale. Her limp hand shakes faster until he shouts his release to the ceiling. I know my brain isn't fully processing what I'm seeing. He's panting, yet her hand is lifeless. My air is cut off as a hand covers my mouth. The hairy back disappears behind the door as Linda keeps her hand over my mouth and pushes me down the hall. When she releases me she doesn't speak. Her black eyes are like orbs. The beat pounds into me as I step out between the red curtains. I feel dazed like I've been sitting in a dark silent room far too long.

Linda's fingers wrap around my forearm as she leads me from the club. Candy looks at me with furrowed brows. I'm pulled into the changing room that's now empty.

"There are rules here. One, that area of the club is off limits unless I tell you otherwise." I nod.

"A closed door means do not enter." She adds.

"The girl. She was dead," I say the words, but I can't really believe it, but that's what I saw.

"The next time you go in there, you can stay there."

Fear skitters up my back and circles around my spine. My dry mouth begs for water. "She was dead."

"That area of the club is for very rich clients who have a certain taste."

Candy enters the room, ready to remove her earrings.

"Get out." Linda speaks while still staring at me and Candy leaves instantly.

"You are sick." Someone needs to report this.

Linda takes a step towards me. "The girl isn't dead. She's pretending to be dead. That's what he paid for. Now get back out on the floor and don't for one second ever even think about going back there again."

Bile makes a burning path towards my throat and I swallow. Her explanation didn't make this any better, it's still sick and twisted and now I'm a part of it.

CHAPTER FOUR

HIM

"We have a problem." Words that are spoken here nearly daily leave Linda's lips. I don't respond as I walk away from Cara's room. The accusation is there in Linda's eyes.

"Or, two problems actually." Linda tilts her head and I stop walking. "Jessie can't dance; she's in pretty rough shape and the boy who hurt her..."

"Mickey," I say.

"Yeah, Mickey. Well...he's here."

I continue to walk. "Good." I have a job in mind for him. I need a new spotter to find me more dancers, the last one started out well, but drugs and drink really screwed with his eyesight as the girls he was bringing back here weren't dancers, not in the least.

"With his dad," she adds.

I glance at Linda over my shoulder and she starts walking with me again. "I'll deal with it," I tell her.

She nods. "Yeah, I think Lady Linda dealing with it will give them an opening for an argument." I fully agree with Linda. "I left them in your study."

We stop outside the door and Linda folds her arms across her chest. She's still pissed about me being in Cara's room. She doesn't like the idea of Cara being here. I've never done this before and change doesn't sit well with her. I don't owe her anything but we have always worked well together and I don't want to jeopardize that.

"We need a new girl, so take Cara."

Linda's hands fall limply to her sides and she tilts her head again, this time with narrowed eyes. She isn't trusting me.

"Seriously?"

"Yeah. I think she will be a great addition."

"They'll eat her up, Gerald."

"You keep an eye on her. Introduce her to the girls and see how it goes."

Linda refolds her arms. "I know what you're doing and I don't think it's wise."

"I'm not looking for your approval, Linda."

Her tongue flicks out, angrily touching her teeth. A reaction that tells me she's getting pissed but she is wise enough to keep her mouth closed.

"Is that all?" she asks.

I hide the grin as she battles with her temper. "No. I want you to let her see a little deeper into the club."

I don't wait, opting to enter the library where Mickey and his dad wait. Mickey is lounging behind my desk, a navy and white striped tracksuit on him, but nothing would take away from his beat up face. His dad has his back to me as he looks at the books on the shelves.

When I close the door behind me they both face me. Mickey grins like I'm in a world of trouble. His father removes his glasses that are perched on the top of his nose.

His split blond hair is highlighted under the lighting of the library. "Are you the man who hurt my son?" He steps towards me and I don't move.

"Yes." I let my word sink in as his father shrugs out of a camel suit jacket and hangs it on the back of the chair that visitors normally sit on. I want to tell him he won't be staying for long, but instead, I allow him to believe that he controls this conversation.

"You're a big man and he's a small boy."

Mickey stares angrily at his father, not liking being called little at all. "I don't think the fight was fair."

"I agree. It wasn't. But the fight between him and Jessie, one of our dancers, wasn't fair either. In fact, it was so unfair, that she's fighting for her life as we speak." Now I step into the room and sit on the chair where Mickey's father had placed his jacket. "Your son could be looking at murder charges."

"Dad, that's bullshit."

It happens so fast, but I have respect for Mickey's father as he strikes his son. "You said you hit her once. You said it was a slap."

"A slap doesn't leave people in comas. He really lashed out at the poor girl." I cross my legs and rest my hands on my thighs; a very non-threatening gesture.

Mickey's father pushes his hair back off his forehead as he steps away from his son. "Did you point a gun at my son?"

"Of course not," I answer straight away.

"You're a fucking liar." Mickey's hopping on the spot and his father strikes him again, this time drawing blood.

This was easier than expected.

"What happens now?" Anger and worry fill his eyes.

"That's up to Lady Linda." I pause and join the tips of my fingers together. "We have the footage of what happened, but we would prefer to not have negative publicity tied to this place." I gesture around the grand library.

He's nodding eagerly. "Just tell me how much."

I grind my jaw and stand.

"I already offered…" Mickey's cut off with another slap and I'm starting to see a picture forming. Maybe he was violent for a reason. My own violence was a seed that was planted and nourished with force.

"How much?" Mickey's father offers again.

"Money won't fix this. But we can come to an agreement."

Mickey's father laughs. "Money fixes everything."

I flash a false smile. "Mickey can work for us." Mickey sits back down into my chair, no longer protesting, he touches his swollen face gently and when he notices me watching, he stops, his eyes are as hard as stone.

"Doing what?"

"Helping around the bar. Think of it as community service."

He glances at his son while shaking his head. "A son of mine working in a bar."

Mickey doesn't hold his father's stare.

His hand is warm as I take it in mine. "I'll let Lady Linda know we have a deal." He doesn't release my hand straight away but moves closer to me until our toes are nearly touching.

"Don't ever put your hand on my son again."

I nod in agreement. I won't. If he crosses me again, he'll be six feet under.

"Be here tomorrow at eight," I tell Mickey as his father slides back into his jacket.

"Yeah." He licks his lip that still leaks a small amount of blood.

His father pushes him out of the room. "I'm glad we could come to an agreement."

"Me too." They leave the study and I straighten my chair and fix anything they have touched.

It's early so the club has only a few clients, all are relaxed and look to be enjoying themselves. I move to the back of the club where I won't be noticed. I can see the back of Cara's head as she watches Wendy dance. I can't see her face but I know she's really watching Wendy, who is a fantastic dancer, but once Cara settles in, she will be the new star. One of the clients approaches her and I step out of the shadows. I keep a watch as he sits down and they talk. I know I'm being watched and I step back into the shadows before meeting Linda's eye, she walks away like she owns the club and I grin.

My attention returns to Cara, after a few minutes she's standing and the outfit fits her like a glove. My body responds instantly. She's divine and I start to regret my decision to allow her here. I don't want to share. She walks away from the man and glances around before she keeps walking. My heart picks up as Damien steps away from the curtains, something he would never do. Linda was following my orders to let Cara see more of the club. Cara pauses at the large wooden door before slipping behind it. I'm not sure who was back there—or what fantasy they're living out—but she's in for a show.

I've just stepped out of the shadows and am spotted by Wendy, who smiles at me and makes her way over.

"You did a great job," I tell her.

She leans against the back of a booth across from me. "I know, I always do." She pulls in a red painted lip between white teeth before pushing off from the booth and stepping close enough to me so we are toe-to-toe.

"We never went for that drink." She looks up at me from under her lashes. The look she is reaching for is innocence, but she lost that a long time ago. As I wait for Cara, I decide to play the game with Wendy.

"You know staff members aren't allowed to date." I move a little closer and can see the pulse flicker in her neck.

"No one said anything about dating. It's only a drink."

"I'm not a one-night stand kind of guy," I say.

Her laughter is loud and rings out across the club. "I won't say I'm not trying to sleep with you because I am." Her hands touch my chest gently and she leans in, the smell of her perfume is over-powering.

I glance at the oak door to see Linda slip through. "I can't say your offer isn't tempting because it very much is..." I trail off and she's holding her breath waiting to hear my answer.

It doesn't take long for Linda to return to the club with a very dazed and pale looking Cara.

A small hand touches my jaw redirecting my attention back to her. "What do you say?"

I lean in close and feel the soft tremble of her body. "I'll think about it," I whisper before sidestepping her. I don't look back as I stick to the shadows and return to the house.

Walking down the hall, I take out my ringing phone.

"You have a meeting at twelve."

I check my watch and it's five to twelve. "For what?" I enter the library. I hadn't seen that in my planner. Opening up the laptop, I sit down.

"A security issue that needs to be addressed about the outside parties. Mary will be there to discuss the details with you." It isn't something I normally do.

I can hear the voices of girls in the background. Linda is still at the club.

"I better go." She hangs up and I leave to make my way into the visitor's part of the house.

The elevator dings as the doors open and I step out into the large open hallway. I sometimes forget how beautiful this house is. The white marble floor under me is polished to a degree that I can see my own reflection. I walk past three large white pillars, large enough to hide behind. My eyes are drawn to three large gold framed paintings. Two are of the forest that surrounds the castle, the middle one, my grandfather. I swore once he was dead that I would burn the castle to the ground. Yet, here I am doing worse to it. I'll tarnish it with all the dirty people and money around me.

"Mary." I greet her with a soft kiss on both cheeks. "Lady Linda explained you had some security concerns."

Mary is in her sixties, her face costs a small fortune, and honestly, it was money badly spent. Her clothes speak of wealth along with the jewelry that drips from her hands. No matter how much work she gets done on her face, she won't be able to hide her age with her turkey-like neck.

"It wasn't as much of an issue, but we had some awkward people with us, who we can't leave out this time either." Money and power both come with their own set of rules. Everyone is fake and you have to mingle with people you don't like—but having sex with people you don't like has me fighting a grin.

"We would like to have extra security there, so, Lady Linda said she would speak with you."

Did she now?

"Of course we can arrange extra security," I say while touching her forearm gently, and she smiles at me, the twinkle in her eyes has me removing my hand.

"I don't want just any security. We've requested you. Some members know you, trust you. So you will be there."

I keep a poker face and pretend that her demand doesn't bother me, but with everything in life there is always an opportunity to fulfill my own needs.

"Can I bring a friend?"

Her eyes sparkle at my request. "Of course you can."

"I'll be there."

I leave Mary and she returns to her group. The women sit around a small table sipping tea and eating cucumber sandwiches like they're the cream of the crop. One thing I've learned about this world of money and privilege is we that we're the bottom of the barrel.

Tonight, I will join in their game. The night will be warm, and the thoughts of having Cara play this game has everything tightening in me. Will I take her tonight? I have to catch her first. All the women will run into the forest, everyone will be masked, and then the men will follow. Whoever you caught, you got to have in the forest—and whatever happened there, stays there. A lot of the women will be old and slow and eager to be caught, but Cara will be afraid. She will run for her life and I will give chase. I can almost taste her panic and it delights me.

I return to the hall and pause once again at the painting of my grandfather. His high chin and thin lips scream all about the asshole he was. How I wish he was alive. I could picture him walking back into his castle only to find a lot of the rooms upstairs hosting swinging parties, private parties, and some pretty twisted things.

Stepping into the elevator his face disappears and I see my own reflection. I have his wide jaw, but that's it. My blue eyes and black hair come from my mother. My mother, who they mistreated along with me, her bastard son. The car accident that took her life was no accident and everyone knew it, but I could never prove what I knew they did. She had shamed their family and she paid for it with her life. Once my mother was gone, no one wanted me, so I was transported to my grandfather and he took all his anger out on my flesh. Pain seeps out and I stop it, allowing my mind to wander to tonight when I will chase Cara through the forest. When I will catch her. When I will take her.

Let the games begin.

CHAPTER FIVE

HER

After Linda leaves me alone in the dressing room, Candy appears. Turning my back on her, I hope she gets the message that I don't want to talk. The chair beside me creaks as she sits in it and twirls while pulling her legs up.

"You okay?"

I spin my own chair so I'm fully facing her now. "No," I answer honestly.

She rests her hand on my leg. "I'm going to make a few guesses, one is that this is like really new to you, secondly I don't think you want to be here."

I go to protest but Candy stops me. "I don't want to know your business, sweetheart. We all have our stories, but I just want you to know that I'm here if you ever need to talk." She pats my leg before fully sitting back in the chair.

"I appreciate it, this place is just ... full on," I tell her.

"You ain't seen nothing yet." Candy winks and drops her feet to the floor. Pulling up her white gloves to her elbows, she rises. I'm staring at this girl in pink wondering if she knows of the horrors that are going on just a few feet away, or if she has ever taken part in those horrid acts. She doesn't look like the type of girl who would do any of that. She looks ... happy.

"You like your job?" I ask, swinging the chair again so I'm facing the mirror.

"It pays well and I've made friends for life. So will you." She smiles at me in the mirror before leaving.

I look so pale. The palettes of makeup in front of me are overwhelming. I'm not one for painting my face, but a bit of blush might take the frightened look away from me.

The rest of the day moves quickly and without incident. My mind can't stop replaying what I saw. I keep an eye on the door, waiting to see the girl walk out, but she doesn't. I can only assume she left while I was out back. The club gets busier and Linda is around less. Today all I have to do is watch the girls dance. My stomach tightens and twists when I think about tomorrow. Will I be made to dance then? Candy has taken the center stage. She's good but not as good as Wendy. The unfortunate part is, Wendy knows how good she is. Her laughter comes from my right. She's talking to two men while sipping a drink that she holds low like she won't be caught.

I don't want to judge, maybe being in a job like this long enough would push anyone to drink.

Candy's dance finishes and when she sees me watching her, she smiles and slips down from the stage. "You want to try?"

Everything in me tightens and she laughs.

"Girl, it's fine if you don't. You look ready to run."

Her laughter loosens some of the tightness. "Yeah, I'm not ready for that."

"Cara." Linda stands by the door waiting for me.

"See you," I say.

Candy gives me an apologetic look. "You take care."

Her kindness is a spark in the night and I'll hold onto it. We leave the club and make our way back to the house. Small back halls that were used by servants allow us to move unseen around the castle.

I hate the feeling that settles across my shoulders as Linda pushes open my bedroom door. I'm waiting for her to leave, but she doesn't.

"You need to get changed. Your master will be here later."

My head snaps up to Linda. "In my room?" I question, thinking about the night he arrived and made me dance.

"Yes Cara." Linda's holding the door handle, ready to close the door. "Like last time?"

"No, not like the last time." She closes the door and I slump down onto the bed. Holding my head in my hands I try to subdue the headache that is threatening to start.

The white material that's laid out on the bed is what I'm meant to get changed into. If I'm not ready when he got here, what would happen? The thought has me rising and picking up the dress. My stomach twists as I hold the light and partially see-through material. It's like something for bed-time. My chest burns as I pick up the scrap of material that's supposed to be underwear.

The bizarre thing about the outfit is the shoes. White sneakers are at the foot of the bed. I strip and start to get dressed, trying not to think about what I could possibly be doing. The white lacy bra doesn't hide much. The stitched material still showcases most of my breasts. My face burns once I have the outfit on.

The final piece is a white mask that covers the top-half of my face. Staring at myself in the full-length mirror, I can't look away, I'm like something out of a fairy tale. A bit of a twisted one but the flow of the see-through dress and the mask were magical, or like a fantasy. I inhale deeply and pull the mask off. Oh, God, am I fulfilling someone's fantasy? *His* fantasy? A weakness enters my legs and I move back to the bed. My frantic mind gets cut off as the door opens and there he stands in all black.

My heart pounds rapidly. Seeing him in the light is more frightening than I could have ever imagined. His wide shoulders fill the door frame. The black material he wears stretches across muscles and a huge frame. His large hands hang on either side of him. The black mask covers all of his face. Gold designs painted onto it doesn't make the overall image gentle, it makes it look frightening.

So this is who bought me. Blue eyes burn into me as they roam my skin. There is nothing I can do to stop this, so I sit still and try not to think about anything.

"Put on your mask."

I shiver as I pick it up and place it over my face. Turning back to him I inhale deeply. He steps deeper into my room filling up the space too much. The hairs rise on my arms as I wait for what will happen next. My mind is conjuring being forced onto the bed. I'm surprised—and a little terrified—when he leaves my room and tells me to follow him.

Each step I take towards the forest has me glancing back at the castle. The lights are distant beacons of safety. Each time I pause he slows down until I catch up. So far he hasn't shown any signs of violence. But what the hell are we doing outside dressed like this? The warm air doesn't stop the shivers that assault my body. Relief swims through me as I hear other voices near the tree line. Maybe it is a party.

A group of maybe fifteen people huddle together. Everyone wears masks. Most of the women are barely dressed while the men are fully clothed. This time I stop walking, dread pools itself in my runners and acts like lead.

"Cara." He's stops again, one large hand reaching out for me to come. I do slowly as I swallow the saliva that has pooled in my mouth. I don't take his outstretched hand but walk to the group of people.

"Great, everyone is here." An elderly woman turns to all of us. The amount of flesh she is showing would make anyone blush. "Everyone is here now so we will start. Remember if you are in trouble, shout 'I'm rich.' We have two security members with us." She points to someone to my left and then directly at my owner.

He's security? I glance at him but he's staring at the woman who's still talking. "So for the newcomers, the rules are simple. All the women run into the forest and whichever man catches you gets to have you."

The ground tilts and the space around me swims. A hand rests on my waist, steadying me. "No." The word isn't heard as the women giggle and get ready to run.

"You need to run, Cara, or I'll just take you here." I hold my breath at his words. A horn blows in the distance. I'm watching everyone run—their squeals of joy—and it's all so distant.

"Run." His word brushes my earlobe like a gunshot and I'm running for dear life.

Flashes of the other women pass me as I race past them. The sneakers make sense now. I run until I get a stitch in my side. Stopping at a large tree, I try to catch my breath. The face of a pig fills my vision and hands reach for me. I scream and back away from the seeking hands. I start to run again.

"That's not fair, I got you." The whine of the man's voice has me running harder, glancing over my shoulder I check to see if he's following. He's not. Turning, I see a flash of black; my heart slams against my chest as he steps out in front of me. I skid to a stop and turn to run back. His breathing fills my ear as he wraps his arm around my waist and pulls me back against him. I freeze. As his hard body pushes against mine, I feel the full extent of his excitement against my backside.

"You will enjoy this," he whispers while moving us slowly back.

I'm shaking my head as my eyes roam the forest, searching for what, I'm not sure. Tightening my eyes closed, I pop them open, hoping this is a dream. I squeeze my body as his hand moves under the material.

"No, don't." I manage to get the words out as he moves both of us down towards the leaf-covered floor. He's still behind me and we are both on our knees, twigs dig into every part of my body that touches the ground. My body feels like it's on overdrive. The material of his clothes against my skin feels harsh. Each time he leans in, his mask rubs my face. His hand has made its way under the dress and he roams his fingers across my ass, his fingers pausing at my back entrance. I can hear the groans and squeals of people close by.

"Spit on my hand."

I glance down at his hand in front of me. I stare at it, not sure if I heard him right. "What?"

"Spit, Cara." His words are right at my ear again. His large erection pushing between my ass as I release my saliva into his hand. A small, shocked squeal leaves my lips as he rubs my saliva along my back entrance. The tip of his finger moves in and I pull away only to have him grip me around the waist and hold me, as he dips his finger in and out. My mind wants to flee to somewhere safe. I don't want this, but each movement pulls me back. I can feel wetness grow between my legs and shame at feeling it burns my face.

"You're so tight." His words have me trying to move again but he pulls me back.

"Don't fight me." The warning is clear as he moves behind me. The sound of fabric being shifted has panic ripping through me. Pulling the dress up and throwing it across my back gives him full access to me. I squeeze my eyes tight as I wait for the pain. His cock brushes my back entrance and he groans as he pushes against it. Pulling back he moves up against me again, this time between my ass cheeks. Heat and wetness flood me again and the shame burns me as I bite my lip. The tip of his cock enters and pain mixes with pleasure, this time I can't keep in the groan that slips from my lips.

"Enjoy it, Cara." His hands hold my waist as he pushes harder before pulling back out.

"No," I say even as my body betrays me. He dips in slightly again before pulling out, his fingers replace his cock, stretching me. I let out a gasp as he enters me again this time deeper, his movements grow faster. Biting my lip I keep in my own pleasure as he takes his cock out and slides it back in the entrance.

"I'm rich!" The shouts of someone in the distance breaks the cocoon of lust I'm feeling. I'm cold as he moves away from behind me and pulls my dress down.

"I'm rich!" The shouts don't sound panicked so I stay where I am until he tells me to get up.

Blue eyes swimming with lust burn into me. "Run back to the house and don't stop until you reach your room."

I nod and turn but he stops me. A hand around my wrist. "This isn't over." His promise sends a shiver down my spine.

I'm running again and this time I want to run away from myself. What was I thinking? I shouldn't have enjoyed that in any shape or form. Tears of shame blur my vision as I walk up to the back of the house.

Once in my room, I try not to look at myself in the full-length mirror. Twigs and leaves are stuck to my clothes. My cheeks flushed from my antics. Tears spill down my face and I hate what I see. I feel so dirty and cheap and I'm not even angry at him. I'm so angry I allowed myself to feel even a tiny bit of pleasure from it.

I need to wash the seediness off me. With no lock on my door, I push a chair under the handle and do the same at the bathroom door before stripping down and getting into the shower. I scrub my skin until it's raw and allow all my shameful tears to fall while promising myself I'll fight harder next time. My core tightens at the idea of next time and I wonder what the hell is wrong with me. A bang on my door has me slamming myself against the shower tiles.

My heart pounds as I listen, but no more noise follows. I wait for another ten minutes before turning off the water and stepping out. Wrapping myself in the towel, I remove the chair from under the bathroom door and step out into my room. The chair I placed against the bedroom door is gone. Fear shoots through me as I glance around the room but I'm alone. His promise that this wasn't over haunts me all night as I toss and turn while trying to find some sleep but it's as elusive as my sanity is right now.

CHAPTER SIX

HIM

My face is sweaty behind the mask and I take ten deep breaths. "I'm rich." The words echo through the forest and I focus on the female voice that cries for help. Removing the mask I follow the voice. "I'm rich." It comes from my left and I see her. A woman in her early forties is sitting on the ground.

"What happened?" I ask while helping her up.

Why was she alone? "Did no one catch you?"

"Yes, I was caught, but Fredrick—like every time—comes too quick." So I was alone when someone robbed my jewelery the same as last week."

So this must have been the awkward person who Mary was referring to. Instead of asking her why she was wearing jewelery or why she wore it after being robbed last week, instead, I ask her if she got a good look at who did it.

"He was young and blond and when he was running away, he displayed a limp." The woman shivers now. The air has turned colder and if you aren't active, you feel it.

"Which way did he run?"

She points off to the left.

I nod. "You go back to the house, I'll take a look."

She smiles and I watch her walk away. I'm not sure I believe her. She doesn't seem that worried about her jewelery, but I start walking in the direction she had pointed. Anything at all that would take my mind off Cara. I see movement up ahead, but it could be one of the other members. Slipping back on my mask, I want to give them the illusion of privacy. A leg clad in white jeans hangs out from behind a tree. I move as quietly as possible, first thinking I can slip by, and secondly wondering what the hell he was thinking of wearing white jeans. The guy's alone, leaning against the tree, holding a ring up to the light. The blond hair and youthful face have me grinning. *She wasn't lying*.

He pulls the ring back when he notices me and stuffs it in his jeans pocket before rising. "What's up, man?" He juts out his chin in my direction in greeting.

"Give me the jewelery back and this will go no further."

"What are you going to do? Ring the Gardaí." He grins and something in the way he smiles triggers a memory.

"Jake? Jake Harper," I say his name as I slide the mask off my face.

He stares at me a moment before his grin turns into a full smile. "Gerald are you fucking kidding me?" He slaps my arm. "What the fuck are you doing out here? You're not banging one of the oldies? You have no idea what I had to watch while waiting to snatch that geebags jewelery."

I glance around me to make sure no one is overhearing this conversation. Jake Harper is trouble with a capital t. But during my childhood, he was the only good thing I had.

I grin. "I'm their security."

He sniggers. "You must have some stories to tell." He leans back. "Jesus, it's been so long."

"Yeah, it has."

"I heard you went to Australia."

I had, but no matter where I ran, I couldn't run fast enough. "Yeah, for a while and I came back. What about you? Besides robbing people."

He laughs. "A little bit of this and a little bit of that."

"Come on up to the house. We can chat."

He narrows his eyes. "Are you sure man?"

"He's dead."

"Yeah, I know, but I just never thought I'd see you around this place again." He shrugs.

"You going to get all sentimental on me?" I quiz and he grins. "I'll also need the jewelry back."

"Seriously?" he digs out the ring and places it in my open hand before we head back to the house. The moment it comes into view I think of Cara.

Instead of bringing Jake to the house I take him to the club. "I've got a few things to take care of, but why don't you go ahead and enjoy yourself. It's on me," I tell him.

"You're fucking with me?" He leans back staring at me like it's his first time seeing me. "This is yours?"

"We'll talk later."

He's already halfway in the door, his eyes bugging out of his head. He's looking at the women and nods. "Okay." He bobs his head to the music as he walks through the doors. Linda glances at me and I nod at Jake, she nods back and I leave her to take care of him.

I leave the ring in the drawer of my desk as I open my laptop to view the cameras. Her room is empty; I click over to the one in the bathroom that's facing the shower. I can't see her through the steamed glass but her outline is there as she washes herself. I watch her for a while until my door opens and Linda steps in.

"Was that Jake Harper you left in my hands?" Linda is never animated but right now there is a spark in her eyes that I haven't seen in a long time, but Jake has a habit of making people feel that way. Closing the laptop, I grin at Linda.

"I found him in the forest robbing our clients."

Linda's laughter is quick, but she fights a grin.

"He called her a geebag."

More laughter bubbles up Linda's throat and it's a weird sound. It's been a long time since I heard her laughter. Her eyes dim like she knows laughing—for her—is weird.

"So what's he doing?"

She sits down in the chair across from me. "I had to stop him from grinding himself on Wendy." She's fighting a smile again. "He's trouble Gerald; you shouldn't have brought him here."

"He's only having a little fun," I say.

Linda shakes her head. "You know what I mean. I'm not talking about him being at the club. I'm talking about him being in our lives."

She's right and I know it. "Let him blow off some steam. We'll have a chat and I'm sure he'll disappear."

Linda looks doubtful but rises, all the earlier happiness is gone, she's back to being her usual business-self.

"I checked on Cara earlier." She tilts her head and waits for me to speak, but I don't.

"She had a chair under her bedroom door that I removed."

She wants to ask what happened, but she won't ask. When I continue to lean back in my chair, she changes the subject.

"We have a problem in the club. The reason I actually came here."

I sit up now. "What is it?"

"It's Wendy. She's drinking on the job again."

I sit forward and place my hands on the desk. "Take care of it."

Linda pushes her seat back in towards the desk. "She won't listen to me, but she might with you. She's our best dancer."

Cara will be. I keep that to myself.

"I'll get changed."

"I'll keep Jake entertained." She speaks as she walks away but I can hear some of the humor back in her voice.

I didn't bother with a tie, only the suit and shirt. The club is alive tonight. I scan all the faces but don't see Jake. He could be in the back. My focus is Wendy. Her red, fiery hair bounces up and down as she laughs while taking a sip of a drink. She's with two clients; one holds her hand lightly, the other touches her leg. Her laughter and easy posture suggests she's loving the attention, but the drink in her hand is saying otherwise. Normally I would fire anyone who was drinking on the job, but there's always an exception and Wendy, in this case, is it.

I wait until one of the men leaves to use the bathroom before I step in.

"Excuse us just a moment." I hold out my hand for Wendy to take and she eyes it wearily, but takes it. "I'll have her back to you shortly." The balding man doesn't look happy as he sits back and drinks his half glass of whiskey.

"Let me get you another," I say and he softens a bit. I stop by the bar.

"Another for the gentleman over there." I nudge in their direction with my head. I've noticed that Wendy hasn't released my hand. "Keep them refilled. It's on the house." That should keep them sweet for a while. We walk away leaving Simon to take care of the two men. Damien's eyebrows raise slightly as we approach but the moment we pass he straightens and faces forward.

The noise of the club ceases as we enter the hallway and I check the doors to find a free room. The second on the left is empty and I take Wendy in.

"Is this where you take advantage of me?" she asks, dipping her head and looking at me from under her lashes.

"That depends."

My answer surprises her and she narrows her eyes slightly. "Don't tease me, Gerald."

Her voice holds a vulnerability that I could use.

"I'm not. I'm worried about you."

The stupid words have her laughing. I'm not worried about her. I'm worried about my profits. Good thing she doesn't know they're mine.

"I am stressed and I could think of a few ways we could destress." She walks towards me like there's music playing, it's slow and seductive. She doesn't stop until her hands rest on my chest.

"You need to stop drinking," I say while removing her hands from me. I don't release her hands even as she tries to pull away.

"That's none of your fucking business."

I tighten my grip. "Linda knows you like me and she asked me to talk to you." Each word is the truth, sometimes adding the truth in with lies helps. It just blurs everything until it all becomes truthful.

She pulls her hands again and this time I let her go. "God, she's a nosy bitch." The drink is giving her courage.

"Don't let her hear you say that," I say sitting on the bed.

Wendy bites her lip and takes a step towards me. "Okay, I'll cut back." She steps up to me and nudges my leg with hers. I widen mine and she steps in between them before sinking to the floor. "You need to do more than cut back," I say.

She exhales loudly. "Fine, I'll stop drinking at the club." She reaches for the zipper of my trousers, but I stop her by taking her face in my hand, making her look at me.

"You need to give me your word Wendy." I dip my head close to hers.

Her nostrils flare and she inhales quickly while nodding her head. The eagerness in her eyes has me smirking.

"I need to hear you say it."

"Fine. I give you my word." She licks her lips while looking at mine.

"You'd promise me anything right now to get what you want." I search her face but she's too focused on my lips, her hands working at my zipper.

My fingers tighten on her face and her eyes snap to mine. "What the fuck Gerald?" She yanks her face out of my fingers, her skin already turning red.

"You're a mess." I stand up and pull up my zipper.

"Fuck you." She's still on her knees as I turn to her. "You walk around like you're better than us, but you're only the help just like us."

I walk back to her and take her by the arm pulling her off the floor. "Go home, sleep it off."

Pulling her arm from my hand, her hands slam into my chest. "Don't touch me you fucking creep. What are you, gay? It's funny I've never heard of you with anyone. Gerald the weirdo."

Her angry words are growing louder, but I don't care about the clients. I just hate hearing her voice. It's irritating me.

"You're drunk and angry that I won't sleep with you. So just go home. I'll ring you a taxi." I offer but my words seem to infuriate her.

She snorts. "Fuck you." She pushes me again with all her force. Both hands slam heavily into my chest. A spark ignites inside me as a window into my past opens but closes just as quickly, like someone quickly looking out a window before pulling the curtain closed. But that glimpse is enough.

A scream of fear more than pain erupts from Wendy. I keep my body pinned against hers as I push her face into the wall. My fingers tighten on the back of her neck.

"You women cry for equality for the good stuff," I say and push her harder until she screams again. She looks at me from the whites of her eyes, pure fear shines there. "But it's okay to put your hands on us, but we can't put our hands on you." I squeeze again.

Tears leak from her eyes. "I'm sorry."

I release her. "If you don't stop drinking, you're fired." I step further away but she still huddles against the wall while nodding in agreement. I straighten my jacket. "You should take the rest of the night off."

She nods again pushing hair out of her face and wipes tears off her cheeks. "I'll arrange for a taxi now."

She only nods again as I leave the room. A few minutes later Wendy arrives back out on the floor. She smiles at everyone until her eyes meet mine, she dips her head and goes out back.

"Gerald! My main man." Jake slings an arm over me and kisses me on the cheek. "You look shit hot in that suit. Like James Bond or something."

"You look drunk," I respond.

He laughs. "Too fucking right I'm drunk. Look at this place." He sounds like an excited child as he jumps on the spot and grins at every woman who passes us. "I'm in heaven." He bites his fist and I can't help but smile at him.

"You met Linda."

He removes his fist from his mouth. "She's always been bangable but now, fuck me, Gerald, she's hot. I'm going to go for it with her."

I laugh. "She'll eat you alive," I say and make my way to the bar.

"Two whiskeys," I say to Simon.

"I don't mind what she does to me. I'm so glad I bumped into you man. This place is my new home."

Simon places the two whiskeys on the bar and disappears to serve other customers.

"You can't stay here," I say, hating to do this to him.

"Why not?" He doesn't sound offended, the drink is helping.

"Linda's orders."

He grins. "She's giving orders now?" Jake picks up the whiskey and knocks it back like it's a shot.

"Let's just get pissed tonight and then figure shit out tomorrow."

I raise my glass to his empty one and take a swing of my drink. Maybe letting loose isn't such a bad idea, it has been a long time since I let myself relax.

"Yeah, let's," I tell him and he drums his hands on the bar while calling for more drinks.

CHAPTER SEVEN

HER

My damp hair has created a wet circle on my pillow. Sitting up, I throw the wet pillow on the floor and take a fresh one from the other side of the bed. My mind won't slow down. Every time I think about what happened in the forest, shame burns my cheeks and coats my chest. I had never felt those things before, the good and the bad. I turn on my side and try to push down the 'good' thoughts. There is something wrong with me for enjoying it. My father always said I wasn't right. Disgust curls in the pit of my stomach. Closing my eyes tightly, I just want to sleep, but my mind won't let me.

I always know when my father gets home from the pub. Every time, without fail, he walks into our small table and chairs, causing them to screech along the tiled floor. The sensible thing would be to move them, but I refuse to help his situation at all. My mother isn't around, he never speaks of her and I never ask about her, so it's just me and my father.

"Cara." His voice holds a note of panic. Normally I would ignore him, but this particular night has me getting out of my single bed and slipping my feet into my carrot-colored slippers.

"Cara." His voice sounds more desperate.

"I'm coming." Pulling the coral dressing gown around me, I turn on lights as I make my way down the stairs. The moment I walk into the kitchen, my initial reaction is to straighten the table, but his shining eyes and open hands have my legs turning to jelly.

"What is it?" I manage to get to him and take his hands in mine. He won't look at me.

"Dad, what's wrong?"

Watery green eyes, still edged from alcohol, plead with me. "I'm in a lot of trouble, pumpkin."

He hasn't used my nickname for a long time.

"What kind of trouble?" Releasing his hands, I fold mine over my chest. The use of my nickname has all my alarm bells ringing.

"I owe a lot of money." He drags out a chair and sits down. Taking a pack of cigarettes from his jacket pocket, he lights one up.

Getting the ashtray off the counter, I slide it across the table to him. Him owing money isn't news to me, I've spent a whole childhood answering the door to debt collectors, telling them he wasn't here when he was really holed up in the sitting room.

"I don't have anything dad."

His head shoots up to me and a look of shock spreads across his face. "I would never ask you for money, pumpkin." There he goes again, using that name.

He stares at me before inhaling deeply and blowing smoke around our small and outdated kitchen. He clears his throat. "I don't have any money, either."

It's there on the tip of my tongue to tell him if he hadn't drank it all, we might have some, but I don't. I decide to be a good daughter and fill up the kettle. A cup of coffee will sober him up and he might figure out a solution in the morning.

"It will be okay dad," I say as I take down two cups. Since I'm up, I may as well have a cup too.

"Cara, sit down."

I hate, with each passing moment, how sober his voice is becoming. I sit down across from him.

"The woman I owe a lot of money to came up with an arrangement."

"There, I told you it would be okay." I reach for his hand and he pulls his away from mine before putting out the cigarette.

"I don't want you to panic." Now he won't look at me. "But..." he's nodding as he speaks each word clearly so there's no misunderstanding. "She is accepting you as payment."

My heart stalls before it kicks up a new kind of pace that's alarming. My hand flutters to my throat.

"It won't be forever." He looks at me now, and whatever he had told himself to make this okay is dwindling fast.

"You did what?" My words are whispered.

"Tomorrow you will be collected."

The laughter that fills the kitchen is tinged with disbelief. "Are you high? Is it drugs now instead of drink?" I rise, pushing his words aside like crumbs. The madness in his words have me breathing a bit easier. It's so crazy that he has to be high.

My father has never put his hands on me, so when my arm is yanked and I'm pushed back into the chair, dread curls around the base of my spine and slowly snakes its way up through me. I hate the look in my father's eyes.

"This isn't a joke, Cara."

Saliva fills my mouth as my heartbeat clouds my ears. "You sold me?"

"I'm sorry. I had no choice."

Bile burns my stomach as my vision blurs. "I don't know what's more hurtful, the idea that you agreed to this madness with someone, or the fact you're sitting here telling me this."

"Cara, pumpkin..."

I blink and my upset is gone. "You do know, Father, that you can't sell me. This isn't the stone age." My words are rising with each word I speak. My own father trying to sell me to clear his debt. It's fucking laughable.

His old hands grip mine and my throat burns. "They will kill me."

Oh my God, he isn't joking. He sold me.

"If you don't go, they will kill me." He repeats.

I rip my hands out of his. "Let them kill you." I'm standing and he's reaching out. Black dots obscure my vision. "Get away from me." I push him and he falls to his knees where he stays.

"Cara, please don't let them kill me." His hands are joined in prayer as his green eyes shine up at me. I'm standing over him as he shuffles forward on his knees. I can't watch this full-grown man beg. His six-foot frame bends around my legs as tears fall onto my cheeks.

"Cara, please." His cries shake his frame.

He clings to me as I cover my mouth in horror at what is happening. "I will never forgive you for this," I say as I step away from him and he releases me.

"Thank you." He can't look at me as he cries into the red and white floor tiles. "Thank you, pumpkin."

DARK

The stairs blur as I race to the bathroom where I empty my meager dinner into the toilet.

I sit up and push back the blanket on the bed. I never thought this is where I would end up. Climbing out of the bed, I pick the pillow up off the floor that I had dumped there. As I throw it on the bed, the room goes dark. I don't move as my heart escalates.

"Dance for me."

I hold still with my back to him. He's close to me. Close enough that I can smell the alcohol on him. I hate the smell. I've been smelling it my whole life. I face the direction his voice came from. The space is pitch black and I can't make anything out.

"No." The word gets lodged in my throat, but I manage to squeeze it out. My heartbeat fills my ears and a cold sweat gathers at the back of my neck as I wait, but he hasn't spoken. He's still here. Will he hurt me? I have no idea of the consequences, but I feel good saying no. I should have told that to my father. I should have told him I wasn't for sale.

"You will dance for me."

Goosebumps break out along my bare arms. Do I dare say no again?

"If you don't..." He doesn't finish his sentence. My eyes prod the darkness, searching for him, for the man who holds my life in his hands.

"What will happen?" I'm being brave, so brave.

His laughter is cruel and quick. A hand curls around my neck. I jerk back startled, but he holds me tightly, cutting off some of the air. When I still, he loosens his hold.

"What do you think will happen?" His rough voice caresses my cheek.

"You'll kill my father."

His sharp laughter has me frantically trying to make him out. It's so dark it's disarming.

"No, I won't do that. I will punish you, Cara and I don't think you'd like that very much." His thumb strokes my neck. I shiver against his touch.

His hand is gone as quickly as it appeared. "Now dance for me."

With shame burning my eyes, I clench my fist and start to dance for him. There is no way he can see me, so I make my feet heavier on the wooden floor so he knows I'm dancing.

Hands touch my arm and I stop. Heat scorches my back as he presses himself against me. Closing my eyes I hold myself tightly, every muscle in my body tightens as I wait. My hair is pulled back from my neck, his breath brushes the bare skin and I shiver again. My thigh pulses as his fingers trail across it pulling my night dress up in its wake. I suck in my flat stomach as his hands reach for the band of my underwear. My vision blurs and I squeeze my eyes tighter as he removes my underwear and stops. I don't move, but open my eyes and try to figure out what is going on. I can make out the bed, my eyes are adjusting, but I can only see the outline of furniture in the room. He's behind me, it's the noise of him removing his clothes that tells me where he is.

"Please don't." I grit my teeth and tighten my legs together as his bare chest brushes my back. He's a lot taller than me. His chin brushes the top of my head as he pulls me closer. My eyes snap open as his erection pulses against me.

Fingers move under the straps of my nightdress and he slides them down my arms removing it until it pools around my feet on the floor. My nails dig into my palms as I stand naked. The urge to cover myself has me keeping my arms at my sides. His large hands roam across my stomach and the muscles spasm at each touch. I exhale loudly as his fingers touch my pussy.

"Don't move." The warning is whispered into my ear as he runs his fingers along my clitoris. I bite my lip at the intrusion and the pleasure.

"Spread your legs." The command has me doing as I'm told. A part of me is excited to see what I will feel next, but a bigger part of me wants this to end. Humiliation starts to raise its head as his fingers slide inside me, it's an instant reaction to step away but he grips my hips and pushes them deeper before taking them back out.

I gasp as he runs his fingers along my back passage. The same fingers that were just inside me, and like back in the forest, he moves us over to the bed and has me bend over. I squeeze my eyes tight as he runs his wet fingers along my ass. Pulling the cheeks apart, he rubs his erection along me and I squirm—only to be kept in place by a large hand on my back. He spreads my legs further apart until it's painful. I don't have time to process the pain as he rubs my ass again before spitting on it. I clench my cheeks trying to get away from him without moving too much, but his hand gets tighter as he pushes his erection against my back entrance. He alters between his fingers and cock, each time going a bit deeper.

Pain rolls up with pleasure and pleasure rolls up with humiliation and I no longer know what I'm feeling. He pushes into me again and I can't stop the groan that leaves my lips. His movements grow faster but I can sense that he is holding back, not going too deep. His cock stretches me and I reach back not sure if I want to pull him closer or push him away. He grips my wrist stopping me as he sinks a little deeper inside me. I groan louder now and a whimper follows, and pain burns, as he pulls out before pushing back in. His pace is quickening. He releases my wrist and returns to holding me up as he thrusts in and out of my ass. My fists curl around the bedspread as he groans and pushes a little deeper. His cock jerks inside me and all my nerve endings feel as if they are on fire. Something in me is building up and I'm waiting for it to erupt. I know I'm going to come and I don't want to; I want him to stop. I want this to be my choice. His breaths grow heavier and I know he's going to come. Biting my lip, I hold back any pleasure that was building inside me until I can taste blood. He releases while gripping my waist and my eyes burn as he goes still inside me, emptying himself. He pulls out slowly, but it still burns and I'm staring at my bed in shock. I don't move even as he steps away. I listen and try not to think as he gets dressed. I don't try to turn around as my bedroom door closes and I'm alone. A sob rips from my lips as I allow my body to crumble on the bed.

CHAPTER EIGHT

HIM

I can't stay in the house. Cara's cries follow me the whole way to the club. I had wanted to stay outside her door and just listen while a small part of me wanted her to stop. Tears were a form of painkillers that our body produced to help ease the pain. I had wanted to ask her if it was physical pain or mental pain that she was feeling.

The air is heavy as I open the doors and the music and sin consume me. I want to sin again. There is power in doing wrong. It's like stepping off a ledge only to find concrete beneath your feet. You took the dive, but you were fine. Men pawed at women they wouldn't get without money, and women danced for men only because they had power. It was a beautiful cycle, one I was proud of creating. Linda ruins my fun when she stares at me, her eyes full of accusation. I pull off my tie as I walk to the bar where Jake's asleep. The moment Simon sees me he nods and flicks a glance at

Jake. I sit as Linda arrives beside me. She doesn't face me but keeps her attention on the room. "You need to sort this mess out." I glance at the mess in question. It wasn't something we normally tolerated. If this were anyone else, they would have been removed from the premises. But Simon had just cleaned around Jake. Linda pulls at the back of Jake's shirt and he stirs. His gaze focuses on Linda as I order a drink.

"Hi sexy. Are you ready to do some real damage?" His words are delivered with a wink, but Linda is beyond pissed as she slams a hand on her hip and increases the hardness in her narrowed eyes.

"I'll sort it," I say while picking up my glass. My words are also a dismissal, one she isn't taking.

"Clearly you're not."

She has my attention now. I face her, wondering where this is coming from.

"Oh, she has you by the balls." Jake reaches out to slap me on the back. I shift making him miss and he lands on the floor.

"I said I'll sort it."

Linda continues to challenge me with a stare but she finally walks away. I knock my drink back as I watch her step into the masses. Any girl who spots her seems to perk up, they dance a bit better, or smile a bit wider. I have her here because she's the best at keeping these girls in line, not for her opinion. Placing the glass on the bar, I get off my stool and stuff my tie in my pocket before picking Jake up off the floor.

"Man, I think I'm drunk." His slurred words have me grinning.

I pull his arm around my neck as I half carry him out of the club. The moment we are out in the hall the music ceases but my ears still ring.

"You've got me into a right mess with Linda," I say as my mind drifts to Cara. Is she still crying? Is she asleep? Does it really matter?

"She'll forgive you, man. She's in love with you." Jake looks up at me through one eye.

His head bobbles back down resting on his chest.

"You've really drank too much," I respond but I don't think he's listening anymore. Linda isn't the type of girl who falls in love. Men fall in love with her and then she smashes their hearts. Thankfully, she isn't my type. *No, you prefer the innocent type.* I quickly silence the voice in my head and pull Jake up as he slumps further down. I'm almost fully carrying him now.

"Help me here, man." He's falling asleep. I tighten my hold on his waist and he wakes up a little, taking some of the weight off me. The walk through the upstairs of the house feels so long because I'm dragging so much dead weight. Jake's fight to help me out is long gone, and he's nearly fully asleep as I open the door to one of the guest rooms. Flicking on the lights, I drag him to the large four-poster bed and drop his body there. Pulling his legs up, I consider removing his shoes, but instead leave the room. I'll deal with getting rid of him tomorrow.

The light in the library is already on, a strip of light pours out into the hall. I hesitate before entering. Only one person would be in here waiting for me. I open the top button of my shirt as I step into the room.

"He's a serious problem, Gerald."

Linda opens the small wooden bar that's been part of this house since I can remember. It was forbidden to touch, so when my grandfather wasn't around I would take the liquor and pour it down the sink. I never drank it, but I wanted him to know that his words held no power over me. His anger at finding more alcohol gone would fill the large house. Servants would be lined up, myself included. But he could never pin it on me. I never drank it and I always put the empty bottles back. It was the only way I could retaliate. His bar was his and his alone, so I made him understand it wasn't. Each beating I took was worth it. To see this God lash out in frustration, everyone thought him such a gentleman, a doting father and grandfather. He was a man in a mask, only a few of us knew that.

Linda pours herself a drink and drains the heavy glass dry before refilling it. Closing up the bar she turns to me, folding her free arm across her small waist.

"He's in bed and in the morning I'll get rid of him." I sit down in one of the brown leather reading chairs.

Linda takes another drink and holds the glass to her mouth, leaving an imprint of red lipstick on the edge. She's thinking, I can see it in how she is looking at me. Those thoughtful brown eyes calculating her next words. I don't have to wait long before she voices what's bothering her.

"I've never seen you drink in the club before. All the girls were questioning it."

"Tell them I wasn't working."

She waves her hand at me before walking to my desk. The pencil skirt and shirt fit her perfectly and I could appreciate it. Leaning against the edge, she places the glass down, but doesn't release it. "Jake was mouthing off about how he knew the owner. How the owner had set him up at the bar."

"He was drunk and he knows you. You are the owner after all." Jake and his big mouth, he always struggled with keeping it shut when he had a few drinks in him.

Linda stares at me before she pushes away from the desk. "For a man who kept things so well hidden and controlled, you're slipping."

I stand up as she passes me, not liking her tone. "It's one night. That's all it is." The words come out harsher than I intended.

"I'm only looking out for you, Gerald." Her eyes soften and Jake's earlier statement has me looking at Linda in a different light.

"I have everything under control. So do what you do best."

She blinks and the hardness returns. "Don't worry, I'll keep making you money."

"Good." I walk away from her done with this conversation.

I'm not ready for bed. It's nearly four in the morning, the club will be winding down soon and reopening at twelve again. Sitting at my desk, I open my laptop and power it on. Cara is asleep in bed, the rise and fall of her chest is steady. My trousers tighten when I think of her. Twice in one night would be too much for her. She is still adjusting. I flick through the rest of the cameras in the club. Most people are leaving, the back rooms are nearly empty except for two rooms. I watch for a while before closing the laptop and going to bed.

"There's a strip club a few miles away from here, most of the girls aren't great but they all come here to work out." I sip the coffee as I stare out over the gym. The platform that hangs over the back of the gym is reserved for me. I pay a decent fee to be allowed to sit up here, or one of my spotters. It's been a while since I've come myself. But keeping spotters is tricky. At first, they love the money—love finding me women—then it's like their conscience kicks in and they want to wipe their dirty hands clean. No one is forcing these women, it's their choice. The owner I have known for a very long time. Barry provides us with all the female information and we sort through it for prospects. He also offers women from any surrounding clubs half-price membership. It keeps his gym full and it makes it easy for me to find new dancers.

"So why are we here?" Mickey's low hanging trousers are making me regret my decision already. The white and blue zippy top looks more appropriate for some street corner. This kid is from a very wealthy background. Why he's dressed like he can't rub two cents together is beyond me.

"Because every now and again a very nice one arrives in and we snag her up." I remove a bottle of painkillers from my pocket and throw two in my mouth before washing them down with coffee. Today isn't looking very bright for picking up new talent. I need it to be. I need to replace Wendy.

"They all look rough to me. Maybe with the head down, and think of the sister."

His smirk slides off his face as I stare at him.

"I'm joking," he says.

I nod. "Did you think I was joking when I pulled my gun on you?" My headache isn't helping this situation. Sitting with this clown isn't my idea of fun.

His face pales. "No, look I'm sorry."

I catch the eye of Barry, who always seems to be here. I can appreciate a man who works hard. Two girls enter the gym and sign in. A few words are exchanged before they step away from the desk. Barry nods at me and I sit up a bit straighter and focus on the girls now. Both of them are blonde, tall and have athletic bodies.

His nod lets me know that they are from the strip club. Both of them start on a treadmill and chat to each other. The tight fabric hides nothing and I can already see them dancing together, maybe sharing a pole.

"What about them two?" I ask Mickey as I point at them with my coffee.

"Great bodies, bad heads." The words slip out of his mouth without him thinking. When he looks at me he starts to apologize, but I cut it off.

"You're right, but once you can identify the great bodies, don't worry about the rest. A pretty face is a bonus, not a necessity." I sit and watch them for another ten minutes. It's mostly for Mickey's sake. He's being fidgety waiting for what's next, and keeping him so close to the line is important, and to know how long it takes before he crosses it is vital.

"So what now?"

Ten minutes is all it took. Yeah, I am really regretting my decision. Standing up, I take the paper that was left here for me. Mickey yanks up his trousers as he follows me to the stairs.

"So what do you want me to do?"

I stop four steps away from the bottom of the stairs. "I want you to talk less and watch more."

"I'm not some low life." His nose curls up as he speaks and I step close to him.

"No Mickey, you're worse than that. You're a rich boy who's terrified of his daddy." I shrug. "So don't tell me what you are or aren't, just do as you're told."

His nose flares but he has the brains to keep his big mouth shut. We leave the gym and climb into my car outside. I'm not sending Mickey up to the girls; I'll get Linda to approach them. I never do, I don't need anyone remembering me for anything, only for security.

"Don't ever wear those clothes around me again," I say before turning the key in the ignition. The car comes to life under us, the hum of the engine gentle.

"What do you want me to wear?" Mickey's still pissed as he speaks to the window.

"Something respectful."

I leave the gym parking lot and make my way back to Slane. I'd told Linda to send Cara to the club again today. Feeling her last night with my hands was more than I could have expected. She's perfect. Even her tears at the end were perfect.

"Like what you are wearing?" Mickey cuts through my thoughts.

"This isn't going to work." I turn off quickly and Mickey clings to the dashboard stopping himself from being jerked around the vehicle.

"I'll wear a suit tomorrow." He still holds onto the dashboard as I turn into the forest and park the car.

"I'm sorry."

I don't look at Mickey but remove the gun from the glove compartment. "Get out of the car," I say as I get out and close my door. He's still sitting in his seat curled up against the door. His eyes follow me as I move around the car. The moment I pull open his door he starts to plead.

"I'll wear anything you want."

"Get out now, Mickey." I tap the hood of my new Audi with the gun and he jumps out with hunched shoulders, like if he makes himself smaller I won't see him.

"I hate clowns," I say as we start to walk.

His eyes dart around the forest and his footsteps slow. I give him an encouraging push forward with the butt of the gun.

"I've a killer headache," I say rubbing my temple. I didn't want to be trekking through the forest all day.

"Here will do," I say and we stop.

He looks around him in a full circle. When he stops at me, his eyes widen at my raised gun.

"It just isn't going to work," I say before I pull the trigger.

CHAPTER NINE

HER

Linda's distracted today. I've been standing in the changing room for the last ten minutes as she talks on the phone. I keep looking at her and my face burns. Did he tell her what he did, what we did? I can feel the heat scorch my neck. Humiliating, she must be laughing at me. I swallow the burn in my throat as Wendy arrives with the girl who was mean to me. Words are fired at each other until Linda holds the phone away from her face and stares daggers at them. Their chat ceases and she leaves. I don't want her to go; I have no idea what to do.

"You're such a fucking liar."

"B, I'm not joking, if you don't shut it, I will shut you up." Wendy removes the hoops from her ears as she threatens B.

B snorts. "Your drunk ass won't do nothing."

Wendy's eyes widen. Slamming the second earring down on the small makeup table, she marches to B. Wendy, is a lot taller, but B doesn't shy away from Wendy. She moves a few paces back before she pushes Wendy back.

"We all know you made that shit up." B's words provoke Wendy, whose face twists into a snarl before she grips B by the hair. I glance around for Linda but she's not in the room and I am not stepping between these two. They are half-bent pulling each other's hair.

"I didn't lie. He hurt me."

B yanks Wendy's hair and my own scalp burns watching them. "He wouldn't touch you. You're just obsessed with him."

They continue back and forth with insults and I keep glancing at the door, hoping Linda will arrive. The door opens and I'm surprised at the level of relief I feel. Candy steps into the room, her pink painted lips open really wide before she looks at me and smiles. "Hi, Cara."

"Hi."

Candy rolls her eyes at Wendy and B and walks around them.

"Say you're sorry." Wendy yells and her fist tightens around B's blonde hair, she has extensions, I can see them coming away from her head.

"That's never going to happen."

I look to Candy who is stripping out of a pink costume and into a silver bikini. Her eyes meet mine and she rolls her eyes again as she clips the bra in place.

"Break it up before Linda comes back." She stands over them but neither is letting the other one's hair go. "Both of you will have to dance bald if you don't stop."

It's like magic. They release each other's hair and stand. Both touch their heads. The door opens again and Linda walks in. She looks at all of us and there is a moment that everyone stares back before they kick into action and start to get dressed.

"Does someone want to tell me what's going on?" Everyone stops as Linda commands their attention. My heart rate accelerates for Wendy. The look of fear in her eyes has my own growing.

Wendy tries to fix her red hair by letting it down while she speaks. "Everything is fine."

"That's not what I asked."

"She's been making up stories about a member of the staff," B says the second half of her sentence while staring at Wendy.

"I didn't make it up." Wendy sounds small and lost and I feel like I'm standing here watching someone being bullied.

"We will talk about this later." Linda speaks before clicking her fingers. "Everyone else get out and start dancing if you want to keep your jobs."

"Linda." Wendy pleads.

I take a final look in the mirror as I wait to hear what Wendy is going to say. My makeup is on perfectly so I'm just stalling.

"I didn't make it up."

"Are you drinking again?" Linda takes a step towards Wendy who takes a step back.

"No I'm not." Wendy notices me and catches my eye in the mirror. Linda watches me too.

I leave the mirror with my head down and go out onto the floor. My body twitches to the music until I make it stop. Only two men are in the club and they look more into each other than they do the girls. Walking around, I hate the pull on my hips.

"Get up." I cover my heart with my hand as I turn to Candy.

"On the pole?" I question as I let my heart rate settle back down. Candy had startled me. But I didn't want her to see it.

"Where else? This is a club." Her blue eyes sparkle as she pushes a soft brown curl out of her face.

Chewing my lip, I stare at the pole. I know I will have to eventually dance, but I don't want to.

"I don't know what to do."

"Why don't you get your cute butt up there and just dance." Candy slaps my behind and I jump away from her, still tender from last night.

My face burns and I try to hide my humiliation. I don't want Candy to question my reaction so I take the three small steps slowly and step onto the stage. It's small and my hands go to the pole. The cold metal under my fingertips takes away some of the heat. I've seen it in the films how they wrap their leg around the pole and swing around it, but I wasn't even going to attempt that.

"The easiest thing to do is pretend you are dancing around a guy you want to sleep with." I glance at Candy and then the pole.

Holding onto the metal rod, I move around it.

"I said seduce him. You look like you're in pain." Laughter has entered her voice and I'm ready to come down, but I can't as Candy climbs up beside me and stands on the opposite side of the pole.

She places her hands on the pole just below mine and starts to slowly walk around it. When she reaches me I move and have to keep moving.

"Now we look silly," I say.

Candy rolls her eyes and grins. "We are two very sexy women dancing around a pole. There is nothing silly about that." Candy's hands loosen, her long red nails now trail along the pole moving up and down slowly. I copy her. Her hips sway a little and I mirror what she's doing.

She brushes her body against the pole before stepping away, I keep copying her until we find a rhythm and I smile.

"You got it, girl." Candy releases the pole and steps off the stage. I stop dancing and glance around the club feeling self-conscious but no one is watching. Swaying my hips, I find my rhythm again and Candy eggs me on. I smile, feeling empowered. Turning my back to the pole, I let my body slide down it before moving back up.

"Girls got moves." I'm surprised by B's praise but I take it. I continue to dance as they go to their own poles. I'm close to the oak door and wonder who's in there now and what they are doing. Facing the pole again, I continue roaming my hands up and down as I dance around it. A young guy with blond hair steps into the club. He rubs his chest while wearing a goofy looking smile. When he catches my eye, he winks at me and starts to walk towards me. I'm aware of each move I make and just want to get down. I break eye contact and when I glance up, my stomach twists, he's standing close to my podium now. His blue eyes dance wildly in his head and they light up even further as Linda approaches him. She doesn't look happy as she takes his arm and tries to walk him towards the door but he stops her. She's talking but I can't hear what's being said. He pulls his arm out of her hand and he isn't looking so pleased right now. I watch, trying to read their lips, but I can't. It all ends quickly and he leaves the club. Linda watches him go before she turns back and catches my eye. With one raised eyebrow she stares at me and I start to dance again.

I wait until she's passed me before getting off the stage. I need to go to the bathroom. Heading out back, the reduction in the noise level of the music is nice. Trying to get out of my costume isn't easy but I manage. It takes me another few minutes to pull the black bodysuit back up. I check myself in the mirror and pause. The door to the second bathroom is slightly open, a pair of purple, sparkly, high heels are visible and I recognize them as Wendy's. The door opens a little more and now I can see her. She's sitting on the toilet drinking a glass of brown liquid. Her eyes clash with mine in the mirror and hers widen.

"What are you looking at?"

I look away from the mirror. "Nothing." I intend to walk past her toilet but she steps out with the glass in her hand and anger in her eyes.

"Are you going to tell?" She steps into my personal space.

"Tell who? And about what?" I know she is talking about drinking since Linda had already warned her, but it isn't my concern or my business.

"You know what. Don't act dumb."

"I won't need to tell, Linda. You smell of drink, Wendy." I feel sorry for her. She had more than just one glass. "Why don't you go home and I'll tell her you are sick."

The impact of her hands on my chest moves me back towards the sink. I'm startled for a moment. "What's your game?"

"I'm only trying to help." Now I wonder why I'm bothering.

"You say anything and I will make being here painful for you." Wendy leaves the bathroom with her empty glass in hand. I rub my chest as I meet my eyes in the mirror. It's hard to hold my own stare.

I do three more dances before Linda brings me back to my room. I'm still red faced when we are alone wondering if she knows what he did to me. She doesn't speak and I'm grateful for that right now. The moment the door closes on me, I'm left alone in my room. I'm facing my bed and my stomach twists. Something is sitting on it. Kicking off the heels, I walk across the wooden floor bare foot and pick up the golden notepad. Opening it, my heart pounds but each empty page has my confusion deepening. Is it to write my thoughts in? I check the bed again and notice a pen and a slip of cream paper that I hadn't noticed before. Picking up the small square of paper, I hate how my hands tremble. I'm terrified and excited to see what's in it. The first thing I notice is how nice his handwriting is. I bite my lip as I take in the curves and dips before I actually read the words.

What is your deepest fantasy Cara?

Seeing my name brings a lump to my throat. It reminds me I'm a person, but right now I'm just existing for him. I'm surviving, not living. Throwing the notepad on the bed, I get out of my clothes and make my way into the bathroom. Instead of a shower, I decide on a bath. Turning on the large golden taps, I tie a nightgown around me as I wait for it to fill. I've left the double doors open and can see the notepad on the bed like a beacon. The question is spinning in my head. What *is* my deepest fantasy? I know the answer and that's why my face burns. Striding across the room, I pick up the pen and notepad but hesitate. There is something freeing in writing it down, my hand shakes a little but I feel lighter. In my own basic handwriting, my fantasy is now there on the first page of the notepad. The actual thought of it coming true has my stomach tightening. Ripping out the page, I glance around the room before stuffing it in the third drawer. I shift my underwear over it so no one will find it. It was my fantasy not his.

I return to the bathroom and remove my nightgown before taking the three steps down into the bath. It's in these moments that I can really pretend that I belong here. I can pretend that this is just a normal day. Taking the cloth and soap that's positioned behind my head, I start to wash myself. When my hand slides between my legs, I slow my pace down and close my eyes. My fantasy of having two men at once is all I can think about now. My hand dips inside me and it feels different doing this in water, so I focus on the outside as I picture them taking turns. They have no faces, no names and they take what they want. My blood roars in my body as I move my hand faster and grant myself relief. Immediately after, I feel embarrassed as I stare out into my bedroom, and at the notepad that's on my bed. I sink under the water, keeping my eyes closed. The water is still under here and it's nice. It's a cocoon of safety from him. Breaking the surface of the water, I push my hair back out of my face. My stomach twists painfully as I think of my father. Is he worrying about me? Is his debt from the club and not gambling like he had said? Is my father one of the men in those back rooms? Is he asking some poor girl to act dead? A coldness has me climbing out of the bath and wrapping the nightgown tightly around my waist. Stepping into my room I don't hesitate as I pick up the notepad and open it to the first page, I write one sentence in it before I close the notepad and leave it on the dresser feeling a bit better. Picking up the cream note that he had left for me, I hold it for far too long, not sure what to do with it. Crumbling it up, I throw it into the bin beside my dressing table. I smile, feeling a bit better that I had made a good decision. Now as I lie down in my bed, I wonder if he will make my fantasy come true.

My deepest fantasy is getting out of this place.

CHAPTER TEN

HIM

A twig snaps behind me and I turn. Jake stares at me before looking at the corpse at my feet. I'm waiting for him to ask what happened—or run—but he does neither.

"You need a hand?" He steps closer and stuffs his hands in his jacket pockets.

"I don't want to involve you," I say as I stare down at Mickey. Blood still oozes from the bullet hole in his head. A pool is growing on the forest floor.

"That's what friends are for, getting rid of bodies." He grins at me before jutting out his chin. "I'll go get shovels."

"Thanks." Jake always pushes boundaries, but I'm not entirely sure how I feel about him being okay with burying a body. This isn't his first time, it isn't mine either, so I won't ask him any questions in hopes he doesn't ask me any. I know having Jake involved is dangerous. He returns with two shovels. Handing me one, he starts to dig a hole. Taking off my suit jacket, I place it and my gun on the ground in front of a large tree. We dig in rhythm, one scoop each and I can see the grave forming.

"You want to tell me what he did? Lie with your woman? Steal from you?" Jake stops digging and leans on the shovel, but I don't stop. I don't want to have this conversation.

"No," I answer while digging faster.

"Come on man. What did he do?"

I pause now and look at Jake. "He ... wasn't dressed appropriately."

I continue digging and Jake joins me, he doesn't ask any more questions.

"I think it's wide enough." We both get out of the grave. It looks a little short but it should work.

I take Mickey under the arms while trying to keep his head away from me. Jake grabs his legs and we drag him over.

"He isn't fitting." We drop Mickey down and his legs hang out of the grave.

"Just bend them back," I say to Jake.

The noise of Mickey's bones breaking has me widening my arms in question.

"What? He will fit now." Jake bends back the leg he broke before moving to the other side of the grave with the shovel.

"Breaking his legs is your only solution?" I ask.

My answer is Jake bringing the shovel down on Mickey's other leg. It slips and slices through flesh. Jake yanks it back taking flesh and blood with it, he slams the shovel down again cutting into the leg. "You shot him in the head and what? Because I broke his legs, I'm the bad guy?" Jake asks from the grave where he twists Mickey's other leg. My gun isn't far away and killing Jake would solve a lot of problems with Linda, and he's already standing in the grave. I could just cover it over.

Jake smiles up at me. "See? He fits." He climbs out and picks up the shovel to start covering Mickey's body.

"Don't be sour over me breaking his legs."

I take the other shovel and decide against killing him. "I'm not," I say as I throw clay on top of Mickey's face. We bury him in silence and when we are done, I move some twigs and leaves and cover the ground to make it blend in with the rest of its surroundings.

"What were you doing out here?" I ask Jake. I wondered from the moment he'd arrived.

"Sometimes those old bags drop jewelery. So I was coming to check."

"Jake, I warned you." I slide back on my jacket and hold the gun, reconsidering using it.

"Yeah and I don't come here while they are at it. I just check the next day." He still holds his own shovel and grabs mine from the ground. "I'll return these."

I tuck the gun in the band of my trousers. I'm not in the mood to dig another grave. "Okay. Thanks."

"Like I said, that's what friends are for." Jake isn't stupid. He'll try to use this for some later dealings, but I'll sort that out when the time arrives.

As he leaves, I take one final look around me to make sure the area doesn't look too disturbed. Kicking some clay across the spilt blood, I return to my car.

A scratch on the hood has me gritting my teeth. It must have been where I had tapped it with my gun earlier. Mickey's phone rings on the floor of the passenger side of the car. Picking it up I look at the caller ID "DAD". I silence it and drive back out of the forest and down alongside the castle.

The further back I go, the more overgrown the land is. It takes a lot to keep the house running and the budget doesn't fully extend to the back grounds. It's wild and overgrown and one day I'll do something with it. Getting out of the car I take Mickey's phone with me and walk for a while until I can hear the river. It runs at the back of the property. Once I reach it, I wipe the phone down and when I reach the gushing water, I throw the phone in. I stand and watch it disappear between the white foaming waves. From this viewpoint I can see for miles in the distance—fields and more fields, along with forested areas that surround the castle. Growing up here was a curse but at moments, with Jake, it really was an adventure.

My throat burns. Bending over, I cough savagely as Jake laughs.

"What is in that?" I hand him back the cigarette he rolled. He takes it and inhales deeply. "A bit of hash, that's all." He offers it to me but I decline.

"Don't be a pussy, man. I thought you wanted freedom." He pushes the cigarette towards me and I take it. Only this time, I take a short drag. My body seems to grow heavier and I give a long exhale while looking at the cigarette. "It's good," I say and Jake slaps me on the back, grinning before taking the cigarette back.

"I love this shit. Me and the boys smoke it all the time. Beats going to school." I envy Jake and his freedom. He has friends that always have his back. Skipping school isn't possible for me. My grandfather would never allow it. I snatch the cigarette back out of Jake's hand and inhale deeply, causing myself to cough.

"No one is going to take it from you." Jake laughs and lies back on the grass.

I was always curious about his friends, and when he told me the adventures they went on, I would pretend I was with them too. I was the leader that was always daring, and didn't care what happened. I was Jake. I had always envied him and even now a part of me still does.

I make my way back to the house, removing my shoes in the wetroom, I wash the soles under the water until all the mud is gone. Leaving them on the floor, I return to my own quarters and change my clothes, I bag everything that I was wearing and place them in the fireplace where I light them on fire.

My phone rings on the desk and I pick it up. "Mr. Norris, Mrs. Conyngham would like a word."

"Tell her I'll be in the tea room in a moment." I hang up and retrieve the ring from my drawer.

Mary is sitting in the tea room and when she sees me she places her cup on the saucer and rests it on the small table. I greet her with a kiss on each cheek. Her thinning blonde hair is brushed back and puffed up to try to disguise the gaps.

I sit down and slide the ring across the table.

"Ah, Ger will be delighted." Mary pours me out a cup of tea, I had no intentions of staying but it would be rude to decline.

"Thank you, Mary." I pour in a small amount of milk and take a sip. Only then does she speak.

"We had a small gathering here yesterday."

I know that. They hired out the top floor that was designed for large private parties.

"I hope it went well," I say.

She smiles, but it's a quick flash. "Of course. When Ger was leaving, she said she saw the man that had robbed her on the premises."

Jake is becoming a huge problem. "Are you sure? That seems rather odd." I sip the tea and she mimics my actions.

"It does seem odd. But she's sure." There's a look in her eyes that tells me she wants to say more but is being careful with her words.

"I will get out all the footage from yesterday and take a look."

Her hand touches my arm. "I do appreciate it, Gerald."

Setting my cup down, I remove my arm slowly. "You are very welcome, Mary."

Mary, after all, is one of our top clients so I'm always gentle with her.

"Are you free tomorrow night? It's going to be a warm night." She gives me a smile and a shrug while raising her tea to her plumped up lips. She wants to use the forest.

"I'm afraid that's not possible, Mary. The forest won't be in use for a while. We had an incident where a member of the public broke his legs while trekking through it, so we are being looked into by our insurance."

"You really need to have a word with Lady Linda and have her close this off to the public Gerald. Riff-raff trailing around the grounds and through the house is beyond me. I don't like having to mix with those types of people." She holds up both hands in disgust as she speaks.

"I will do that Mary, and I'm sorry for any inconvenience this may cause you."

"A big inconvenience. You should say that to Lady Linda too. A discount would soften the blow." This woman could buy and sell us, but if she needed to feel like she controlled this situation, that is fine by me.

"I will make sure you get a generous discount."

Mary smiles and rises as I do too. I kiss her on both cheeks. "Always a gentleman, Gerald. I hope Lady Linda knows how lucky she is to have you as a loyal staff member."

"Yes she does." I leave her and enter the hall, my eye immediately drawn to the painting of my grandfather. My whole body tightens and I feel he watches me all the way to the elevator that I take up to my quarters.

Once I'm in the library, alone, I open my laptop and rewind the tapes. I stop and hit play, her room is empty, but my note still sits on her bed along with the notepad. I flick to the second screen, she's filling the bath up. She looks contemplative as she stands and walks to the bed. I can't stop the jerk in my pants as she writes something in the notepad. I can't see but I look forward to reading it later. She tears the page out and stuffs it in the drawer before getting into the bath. I'm ready to switch off the laptop and make my way to her room when she starts washing herself. Her head rolls back in pleasure as she touches herself. My trousers grow tighter as I sit there and watch her release. I need her...and I need to know what she wrote on that piece of paper.

Before going to her room I unplug the fuse on the fuse box knocking off all power to her room.

CHAPTER ELEVEN

HER

I am aware when the lights go out; the darkness behind my eyelids grows even darker. Searching the darkness for him has my heart rate escalating. I can hear him breathing. I know he's here. The notepad and the question about my fantasy has my stomach tightening. Is he here to find out what I wrote down? If he sees it, will he make my fantasy come true? I shiver and tighten the nightgown around me. All the hairs rise along my naked body beneath the nightgown.

"Did you get my note?" His deep voice has me sitting up straighter now, I let one leg dangle off the side of the bed as I search the darkness for him, following the sound of his voice.

"Yes." My voice sounds so small, like it's been consumed in a crowd.

"Tell me your fantasy, Cara."

I let my foot slide down the side of the bed and touch the cold wooden floor to take some of the heat away from my body.

"To go home." My voice trembles on the words.

"Follow my voice."

I'm standing now, taking two steps towards his voice.

"We both know you don't want to go home."

My body jumps, he is so close, his words have me swallowing down my confusion. "I do want to go home," I tell the darkness, but my words fall flat. I don't want to stay here and be used and humiliated, but going back to my life, to my father, to the struggle, that I don't want. I know what it means to be hungry and cold. Here I don't have to worry about that. Yet, I have new worries. I am afraid of what this man could do to me. What he intends for me.

I freeze as large hands touch my neck. His breath fans across my forehead and I close my eyes. Fingers trail along my arms until they reach the band of my nightgown where he pulls the rope, allowing the material to open wide. My face burns and I close my eyes as he pushes the material from my shoulders and it pools around my feet on the ground.

His hands return to my neck, the heat sears into me. He moves my head to the left and right gently but completely in control. "I could kill you so easily." His whispered words in my ear have the blood and heat draining from me.

"I want to break you, Cara." He whispers in my other ear and I hold my breath, my heart is pumping blood too quickly around my body, making me light-headed. He releases me but his hands don't leave my body. Light fingers flitter across my stomach and stop at my pussy. I want to tell him not to, but I'm starting to learn that it's pointless. His hands move between my thighs and I tighten my legs.

"Open them."

I spread my legs and close my eyes. My body reacts to his touch. My core starts to tighten and tremble instantly. I hate it. I hate myself for wanting him, for wanting more. Fingers dip inside me. My shoulders tighten when he removes his fingers, I know they are slick with my excitement. My throat burns with disgust as my body burns with a want I can't explain. His hand touches my lips.

"Taste yourself." He whispers.

I don't. I'm frozen. His hand leaves my lips and the sound of him sucking his fingers has my eyes widening. I can make out his outline now as my eyes adjust to the darkness. His large frame scares me. He's moving, removing his clothes. A part of me is screaming to run for the door, to get out while I can. He returns to me taking my throat in his hands. His large erection brushes against me and jerks as he tightens his hold on my neck. My hands go to his arms and he eases his hold but doesn't release me as he pushes me back towards the bed, forcing me to sit. I'm released from his hold. A startled yelp releases from my throat as his lips connect with my thigh. I try to close my legs but his large hand pushes them open, his other hand presses on my stomach, pushing me back until I'm lying flat with my feet dangling over the bed. I tell myself to pretend that I want this. To pretend that this is okay. His tongue flicks out and my eyes snap open at the sensation. I am a virgin in every sense. His tongue moves deeper and my hands move to his shoulders wanting more and he gives me more, his tongue flicks and jerks before he stops. His hands grip my thighs as he moves up my body, and I think to myself that this is it. I'm going to lose my virginity like this, but he keeps moving until he's sitting on my chest before he bends over me, his cock touches my lips and I don't move.

"Take it," he commands.

Closing my eyes, I open my mouth and allow him entry. He dips it in and out. Pushing it further down my throat until I start to gag. I try to push him away but I can't. Tears leak from the corners of my eyes as he pushes himself into my mouth again before removing it. He's off me quickly and I'm trying to catch my breath when he pulls my legs wide and places himself at my opening. The warning is on my lips to tell him I'm a virgin but he pushes himself in. Pain sears my body and I shout out, he groans and pulls out. I want to tell him to stop, but it's like my body is no longer my own. He pushes in again and I look away as I grip my bedsheets. He isn't holding back, his pace quickening and I just want this to end. Hands wrap around my throat and I'm facing him with open eyes as he moves even quicker. The pain mixes with something more that I don't want to identify. The air becomes thinner, and then his movements become frantic. He groans loudly, thrusting in and out of me as his hold on my throat tightens until I think I'm going to come.

After he leaves, the lights come back on and with it a flood of emotions. There is blood on the white bed sheets. Frantically and through a cloud of tears, I pull it off and walk slowly to the bathroom. My body isn't allowing for any quick movements. A sob pulls from me as I clean the blood from between my legs. The mirror I glance up at has a girl looking back at me, mocking me for being so disgusting. I had wanted him; I didn't try to stop it. It's my fault.

Turning on the bath, I step down and hold the sheet under the water and start to scrub, but my blood isn't disappearing. The splash of the heavy sheet onto the tub isn't enough to disguise the noise of someone entering my room. I don't think but jump out of the bath and wrap a towel around myself as Linda steps into the bathroom. I watch as her eyes take everything in from the bedsheet to my shaking hands. My face burns with humiliation.

"I can see you aren't up to dancing." Her voice doesn't hold any emotion and it allows me to gather myself and step out of the bathroom and away from the bloodstained sheets. My control slips as I stare at the tossed bed. Tears make a pathway down my face.

"The only way to free yourself is to take control."

I turn to Linda and swallow some of the emotion.

"If you don't take control, he will keep taking until there is nothing left." Her words hold some form of emotion, hurt, regret, and understanding maybe.

"I want to leave this place," I say wiping my nose.

Linda tilts her head sideways. "That's not going to happen. I'll leave you for tonight and you can come to the club tomorrow."

Fear has me stepping to her. "Don't leave me." I feel so weak saying it and I don't blink as I wait for her to answer me.

"He won't come back tonight." She turns and leaves me and I blink, tears falling down my cheeks. She is right, he doesn't come back, but sleep isn't something that comes either. My mind is replaying the whole thing over and over again.

The next morning Linda arrives and I'm already dressed and waiting. She raises an eyebrow in surprise when she sees me, but she doesn't say anything. After a sleepless night and hours to think about everything, I decide I don't want to be a victim, I'll take control. The club doesn't scare me and seeing Candy and the girls is actually starting to become something I am looking forward to. I still feel fragile, but I won't let him win. The next time he comes to me I will tell him no, I will fight him; I will take back my control.

"You can go straight out onto the floor." Linda dismisses me and I don't linger in the changing room. Something tugs at my chest when Candy smiles at me from across the room. Can I tell her? I want to. I wave back, but maybe she's as much a captive as I am. The club, once again at this time of the day, is empty. I count five men, all of them watching Wendy dance. I turn and watch her too.

"She has moves. But don't ever tell her I said that." Candy bumps shoulders with me in greeting and I focus on her smile and mirror it.

"Are you dancing today? Give her a bit of competition."

Candy's compliment has me blushing and I shrug. "I'm not sure. Linda just told me to go out on the floor."

"You should use this time to practice." Candy nudges me towards the empty pole I danced around yesterday.

"You take this very seriously," I say. She walks with me to the pole.

"It pays the bills and more." She winks and departs as I climb the three steps up onto the stage. I don't think about last night. I don't think about anything, I just dance. I dance with my eyes closed and when I open them I notice I have gained the attention of two men. I slowly turn my back on them as I continue to dance. Wendy moves across the room, hips swaying dramatically. She doesn't stop until she reaches the oak doors. I slow my dance as I watch her push the door open and she slips through. I stop dancing and slowly get off the stage ignoring the man who's walking towards me. I'm looking for Wendy but can't see her.

I find Candy and B out the back laughing. I want to ask about Wendy going into the back rooms but I don't want to with B present.

"Hi Cara." Candy rotates in a circle on the makeup chair. "We are just talking about wardrobe malfunctions that have happened."

B isn't laughing anymore, she's watching me full of suspicion as I stand awkwardly.

"Relax, B. She's cool."

I appreciate Candy vouching for me, but I don't feel comfortable with B either, not after her non-friendly welcome.

"B was dancing one night and she was pretty hot, myself and Wendy stopped to watch her." Candy is grinning as she speaks.

"Not this again." B's trying to sound angry but as she faces the mirror, I can see the amusement in her eyes.

"Yes, this again. So..." Candy fully faces me. "She's wearing these lycra hot pants, black, real tight. Too tight." Candy laughs and B swings around in her own chair holding a hairbrush.

"Girl, they were really nice pants." She brushes her blonde hair out.

"Yeah, so tight they ripped." Candy finishes while laughing. "She had nothing underneath. Everyone got more than they paid for."

I smile. Candy's laughter continues and there's something warm about it. It's the type of laugh that makes you want to chime in.

"That fool really messed up my extensions." B pulls a handful of loose strands from her head. "Did you hear the lies she was spouting?"

Candy nods while applying lip-gloss to her already shiny lips.

I feel silly standing here, but I don't want to go back out on the floor. This feels somewhat semi-normal.

"Yeah, she said Gerald hit her." Candy pouts in the mirror.

My body perks up. Gerald. The doctor had used that name before. It wasn't possible that he was here in this club.

"Gerald?" I quiz, hoping I don't sound strangled.

"Yeah, the security man. Big guy," Candy says.

B grins. "Hunky, mysterious. Sex on legs." She laughs and Candy nods.

"Is he the guy at the red curtains?" My question has both of them sobering up.

Candy swings around so she is facing me. "No, that's Damien. And keep away from the red curtains; it would break someone like you." Pain is in her eyes and I want to tell her I was already back there and saw what happened, but I don't. Instead, I nod.

"You wouldn't miss Gerald. He lurks in the back of the room," B says.

Now all I want to do is go out on the floor and see if he's out there. I'll finally get to see him. I feel sickened at my own excitement.

"We better get back out." Candy touches my arm as she speaks. "You okay?" she asks and I force a smile.

"Yeah."

I return to the floor and serve drinks this time, all the while searching the club for the elusive Gerald. I don't see him. Two other security men linger around the room. One being Damien, the other is too small and slim to be Gerald, if that is really his name.

Linda arrives on the floor an hour later. She beckons me towards the main doors and I know it's my time to go back to my room. I'm frozen for a moment, it's a sad day when I want to stay at a dance club.

Linda doesn't speak and neither do I. What is there to say? The only thing that is on my mind is to take control of this situation and that means standing up and saying no to him. I hate the feeling I get when I step into my room and see clothes laid out on my bed. I stare at the leather attire as Linda closes the door behind me.

CHAPTER TWELVE

HIM

The slam of the library door has me sitting back in my chair. Linda's heels click heavily as she approaches my desk.

"What are you doing with that girl?" Her hands rest on my desk as she leans in. Her eyes hold anger and pain. I understand why, but this isn't the same thing.

"None of your concern."

She pushes away from my desk while she brushes her hand across her forehead. "You're grooming her," her voice is low as she looks around the library.

"I said it's none of your concern," I repeat myself, raising my voice slightly in hopes of snapping her out of this.

"I get it with the dancers, and the back room, and the parties. I do, Gerald." She's leaning back, and her eyes are pleading with me. "But this girl? I don't understand," her voice softens.

"I'm not asking you to understand."

She's standing up fully again and I don't like her losing control like this. "You're getting too close to her."

Her laughter is bitter. "I don't even speak to her. I just don't like what I'm seeing."

I clench my jaw. "You don't have to deal with her anymore then."

"No, but I have to deal with the questions from her father. Asking me about his daughter."

"I'll deal with him," I tell Linda, just wanting her to leave. She is fragile-looking, and I am busy.

"How? The same way you dealt with Mickey."

I stare at Linda and she folds her arms across her chest looking unsure now. She is stepping on thin ice with me.

"I don't want that girl groomed," her voice is small, ghosts heavy on her heels. I can see it in her eyes. She could chew her own pain. It is that heavy.

"She is being groomed for the back rooms," I answer honestly, something in my stomach jerks.

"It would break her, she's too fragile."

"She's stronger than you think. I think she would enjoy it."

Linda looks at me from the corner of her eye as she half turns away trying to hide her own pain. "She doesn't enjoy it, Gerald. I saw her yesterday. I saw the state she was in."

"Take some time off, get yourself together and then come back." I face my laptop to dismiss her. She's a mess and has no idea what she is talking about. Cara's body responded with eagerness, I remind myself. Linda is too caught up in her own past. This isn't about Cara, it's about her.

"No, I'm fine."

I exhale loudly and look back up at her.

She straightens. "I am fine, Gerald. Wendy is making a racket about you putting your hands on her. I think it's best you fix it." Slowly, very slowly, Linda is returning.

"Is she still drinking?"

"Yes." Linda's answer is instant. "Did you sort out Jake?"

I rub my forehead before looking back up at Linda. "I'll sort it. Is that all?" I don't think she can pile any more on top of me.

"I just have one more question about Cara."

"Linda..."

"I promise it's the last one."

I sit back in the chair and join my hands together. "Fine, one question." If this is what it takes to make her move on, so be it.

"How did you pick her?"

I grin. "How did you know I picked her?"

Her lip tugs up slightly but her eyes are dead. "You first."

"She used to visit the castle. I spotted her one day on the camera and I just knew. She was innocent and teachable. I could see the potential." She had been staring at the painting of my grandfather. She was smiling up at it and I could see it. She wanted more.

Linda drops her arms at her side.

"Now you, how did you know I picked her?"

"Her father had no debt with us. He was a drunk that you brought here one night and then he owed us a small fortune. I knew when you suggested his daughter as payment, that there was more to this."

It was too easy, but I was sick of the same thing all the time. I wanted a challenge and Cara was perfect. *Is* perfect.

Linda's shoulders fall forward.

"Are you satisfied now?" I can tell she isn't and clench my jaw.

"Yes." She nods before leaving the library. Linda is broken to the stage—she is perfect. She shows barely any emotion and her moral compass didn't exist until now. I hate it. Money is power and power is everything. Nothing else should matter. Not our past, not other people.

I'd been stealing from my grandfather from a very young age. The value of money—I am very aware of it. It has its own power. People respect you if you have it. It gives you power, it gives you the right to hurt people, belittle people without consequences. People love you because of it. They envy you because of it. I wanted money so badly that slowly I gathered it by stealing from right under my grandfather's nose. He noticed. He counted every penny, but I was always careful not to get caught. He knew deep down it was me, but he had no proof.

The old sheds out in the back was where I hid it all. Three loose floorboards discovered while smoking one day became my saving grace. I'd hated my life and when I found the empty space under the shed, I decided I would fill it, I wasn't sure with what but when I saw the power of money, I decided that's what I would fill it with. Each note made me taller. Yet when the hole filled up, it wasn't enough, I couldn't stop the addiction. I grew clever at stealing things, it went from cash to items and then documents that grandfather kept. By the time he died, it was all in my name. It was all mine. All the money. All the power.

My ringing phone pulls me out of my thoughts. "Mr. Norris. We have a situation. Mrs. Conyngham wants a word." She is becoming a nuisance.

"Can it wait?"

I can hear Marcus asking her if she can wait.

"No, this is very important," Mary sounds agitated.

"I'm on my way," I tell Marcus and hang up. This better be important.

Mary, another woman, and Jake are waiting for me. I can already see what has happened.

The brown-haired woman who I can assume is Ger, the owner of the jewelry, steps up to me with a demanding tone. "He is the thief who took my jewelry."

"Okay Ger, let's take this down a notch." Mary touches Ger's arm and it seems to calm her slightly. I glance at Jake who seems to not have a care in the world. That needs to change.

"Yes, I think if we all calm down. We can talk out back." I don't want anyone over-hearing our conversation.

"He's a thief," Ger's voice rises.

I nod. "We will discuss it all in here." I open the door to a side office that is rarely used. Three Queen Ann's are scattered around the room. Mary instantly sits down. Jake stands close to the fireplace and when Ger steps into the room, she looks around her.

I close the door. "So what are you going to do about it?" Ger asks straight away.

I look to the accused. "Did you take this woman's jewelry?"

"I just said it was him." Ger steps closer to me, demanding my attention.

"No, I didn't. She's a mad bitch."

Ger's eyes widen and Mary's rise into her hairline.

"How dare you?" Mary turns on Jake.

I open my hands wide to try to calm this situation down.

"I believe you," I tell Ger and she bristles in satisfaction.

"So what are you going to do about it?"

"You will be compensated and I'll ring the Gardaí."

"Compensated how?" Mary rises and the gleam in her eye has my lips tugging.

"However Ger wishes."

Mary steps closer. "I have been affected by this too."

Ger looks doubtfully at Mary.

"I will let Lady Linda know."

Jake snorts a laugh. "Lady Linda. She's a far cry from a lady."

Both women gasp and I don't know if Jake is dumb or if he thinks this will all go away. Either way, I need to get these women out of here.

"You ladies should get some refreshments while I deal with this." I glance at Jake who's turned his back on us. He's picked up a candle holder, turning it upside down to see if it's stamped.

"Are you sure? Maybe we should stay as witnesses." Mary half whispers but I hear Jake's snort.

"Thank you, Mary, but I'll be fine." It feels like it takes a long time to get both women out of the door.

"I think we should clip the two bags." Jake grins.

"You shouldn't think Jake. This isn't your place to think. And I don't go around killing people. Those two bags are very rich clients that keep these doors open."

"You do kill people." Jake places the candle holder back on the mantelpiece. His earlier grin gone.

"I need you to leave," I say. I shouldn't have ever brought him here.

"Just like that. I'm thrown aside for your rich friends."

"We aren't kids anymore." I clench my jaw. I should have killed him when I had the chance.

"You really want me to go?" I didn't like the way he asked the question.

"Yes."

"Okay." Jake glances around the room as if it's the last time he will ever see it.

"I didn't want it to end like this."

He holds up his hands. "No need to explain. I get it." He walks past me and brushes his shoulder against mine. "Go play with your rich friends." The door closes behind me and I ring Marcus.

"The blond man who just left the office, make sure he leaves the property."

"No problem." Marcus hangs up and I slip my phone back in my jacket pocket. I knew it wasn't that simple with Jake. I just hoped he didn't push me so far that I had to kill him. If he disappeared now, I would let him walk away. I also need to move Mickey's body, he knows where he is and I can't allow that to be held over my head.

I arrive at the club. My number one goal is to find Wendy. She's laughing with one of the other girls but when she glances my way her smile slips. I look away from her and glance around the club. It's getting busy and I easily get lost in the crowd while keeping my eye on Wendy. She's keeping an eye on me too. She gets up from her seat and walks along the front stage. I move along the back wall until she disappears out the back. I wait for another ten minutes and she reappears searching the club. Once her eyes meet mine, she ducks her head and pulls up her shoulder bag before leaving the club. I count to thirty before I make my way after her. Staff park behind the club and that's where I find Wendy with car keys in hand. She hasn't opened her door, her back is still to me.

"I'm sorry."

I nod to her back before walking to the front of her car. "Sorry for what?" I ask her and she looks up at me, her eyes clouding.

"I'll tell everyone it was a lie." Her mouth twists as she fights to keep her tears down. A pity she didn't think about that before.

"It's a little too late for that."

Tears fall from her eyes. "Please Gerald. I messed up."

Fear blossoms in her and I tap the top of her bonnet before walking away. "You're right, Wendy. You messed up."

"Please Gerald. I'll do anything." She calls after me but I keep walking, feeling confident that she understands to keep her mouth shut in the future.

I stay outside and slowly make my way to the forest. I need to make sure I can find Mickey's grave easily later tonight in the dark. I'll dig him up then. The sun is starting to dip, but it's not dark enough yet. Thankfully, not many people are around, I pass only two tourists who are walking around the grounds. I had Marcus place tape at the entrance of the forest to make sure no one enters. Lifting up the tape, I duck under it and glance behind me to make sure no one is watching.

I arrive at the site where I buried Mickey. The ground looks the same. But later tonight it might not be as easy to find. Picking up a large rock, I place it on the grave as a marker. Throwing it down, the breeze shifts some of the leaves and display's heavy footprints, the tracks look like runners and that's something I don't wear but I know who does.

God damn it Jake.

He is going to force my hand. Leaving the forest, I make my way back to the house. Later I'll deal with this, but right now I have an appointment to keep. It's one I am very much looking forward to.

CHAPTER THIRTEEN

HER

I never noticed how much creaks and noises this house made. Sitting here waiting for him to come has me hyper aware. The leather costume that he left out for me is still sitting on the bed. I've tidied over the room several times and each minute feels like an hour. I just want him to come so I can get this done and over with. I am going to take control just like Linda said. Every time I look at the outfit my stomach twists. I'm up and opening the drawer that I left the piece of paper in with my fantasy written on it. Moving all the clothes both ways doesn't make a difference, it's gone. I quickly open all the drawers dumping the contents onto the floor, but the note isn't here. My heart pounds as the lights go out. Closing my eyes, I tell myself to be strong.

"You're not wearing the clothes I left for you."

I don't bother searching the darkness this time. "I'd hardly call them clothes." My voice shakes slightly and I hate it for betraying me.

"Everyone is very brave today." I had no idea what he meant.

"There're other girls locked up like me?" I hate the sting of jealousy I feel at that thought.

"Put on your outfit."

My heart thumps painfully against my chest, threatening to break free. "No."

His hand brushes hair behind my ear, the hairs rise on my arms at his touch. "So brave. So defiant." A cloth covers my eyes and I raise my hands to grip it. "Leave it." Something in his voice has changed.

My hands flutter to my sides as he ties the blindfold at the back of my head. I'm surprised at the gentleness when he takes my hand in his. I know when we leave the room, the light changes but I still can't see. I'm aware that if I pull off the blindfold, I'll be able to see him.

We stop, and the ding of an elevator has me looking around at the darkness. "Where are we going?" I ask as we descend.

He doesn't answer. A few seconds later his hand takes mine again. Mine feels so small in his. His skin is soft and warm and I know I should be repelled but I'm not. We step out of the elevator and start to walk. It's colder now. We pause and a door opens.

"Hello." A male voice that I don't recognize has me pausing and tightening my hold on Gerald's hand.

"Don't be afraid." His words are closer now and I take a step back. I can't go far as Gerald still holds my hand. His hold on me tightens.

"I want to go back to my room." I hate how small my voice sounds.

A hand I don't recognize touches my face and I try to move away from it.

"It's okay." Gerald's voice pulls me towards him as he starts to walk again. My hand touches the silky fabric of a bed. My stomach twists and tightens as I sit on it, Gerald lets my hand go and I feel like I'm falling down a rabbit hole. Lips touch my neck on both sides. My hands grow slick with sweat.

My fantasy. He found it. He's making it come true.

A panic in me rises as I'm pushed back onto the bed. Lips trail down my neck while hands roam across my chest. I gasp as my trousers are opened.

"Lift up." It's Gerald's voice and I raise my bum off the bed as he pulls my trousers off. Hands touch my bare flesh and make their way between my legs, touching and gently rubbing the outside of my underwear. I know the moment Gerald touches my face. I know the feel of his hands and I'm not sure if I should be horrified by that.

"Let yourself go," he whispers into my ear, before placing a kiss behind it. It seems like such a personal thing to do. My legs are widened and the other man moves in between them, his thighs brush against mine. His erection brushes against my throbbing privates and I turn my head to the left, towards where Gerald is. His lips still brush my neck as his fingers work on the buttons of my shirt. The moment he has it open, his fingers trail down my stomach, past my belly button and to the band of my underpants. Large hands touch my breasts, the erection solid against me. I bite my lip as my bra straps are slid off my shoulders and my bra is pushed down. I groan as Gerald takes my nipple into his mouth. Fingers run under the band of my underwear and touch me. I jerk as electricity shoots through my body.

Gerald's tongue strikes out, my nipples harden and when his teeth graze it, I think I'm going to come off the bed. The man between my legs leaves and I feel the loss immediately, but it doesn't take him long to return, as he removes my underwear. His large erection is placed at my opening but he doesn't push through. Instead he takes my other breast in his mouth and sucks. Gerald disappears and I can hear the ruffle of clothes. The bed dips beside my head and something warm touches my face. Raising my hand, I touch the meaty cock. My heart pounds as Gerald's fingers sink into my hair and he directs my mouth closer to his cock. I keep my lips pressed together and my body dulls, it's like someone has doused me in cold water. I reach out to push the man away from in between my legs.

"Shh it's okay," Gerald whispers close to my ear as he kisses my neck. It's an ember in the dark, and it sparks to life again as fingers touch my private parts, separating the flesh before dipping in. I arch my back and move back down as Gerald's mouth consumes my breast. Fingers touch my ass and it's all too much. I want them to stop. I want them to keep going. Gerald's hands take over from his tongue and when his cock twitches against my lips I open my mouth and he enters slowly. I pause as a cock enters me, it's painful as it stretches me but the movement in and out turns the pain to pleasure. My tongue flicks out and licks the top of Gerald's penis, I hear him groan and it makes me feel powerful. Everything stops and my body screams no. Hands direct me until I'm crawling across someone. The moment the hands touch my hips I know they are Gerald's as he positions me on top of the other man who directs his erection into my opening. I don't move as he pushes himself into me, his hands going to my breasts. Squeezing my nipples, I let my head fall back onto Gerald's chest. Warm liquid coats my ass and Gerald pushes his fingers inside as the other man finds a rhythm inside me. Gerald's hands hold my neck from behind as he thrusts the tip of his erection into my ass. I'm being stretched everywhere, lips touch my neck before teeth graze the sensitive skin. I find myself rocking to the rhythm the three of us have created.

Gerald pushes deeper into my ass and my hand reaches behind me for his thigh, wanting him deeper. Inside my pussy the other penis feels like it's growing bigger, filling me, stretching me. Our rocking grows faster. I bite my lip as my nipple is squeezed, a sensation is building in me and I don't want it to end. Gerald pushes deeper into my ass, his teeth sinking into my skin. Every part of my body is screaming for release, every nerve on end. The pace quickens and when Gerald groans in pleasure along my neck, I let my own pleasure slip through my lips. It encourages both men to go deeper, to go faster. Hands tighten on my neck cutting off some of the air, and I throw my head back wanting to give both men access to every part of me. Everything is too much, I want my release, but I also don't want this to end. Gerald's breathing quickens along with the man under me, who pounds into me heightening my arousal, my wetness is dripping from me. I can feel it on the inside of my legs.

"Come for me Cara," Gerald speaks as he sinks fully into me and I groan and cry out as the man under me pounds into me and stops releasing himself. I'm so close as Gerald's hands leave my neck and find their way into my hair. Pulling my head back painfully, he pounds harder, the pain sears through me but the pleasure isn't far behind as he continues to slam into me. Fingers prod at my clitoris and I can't stop the onslaught of electricity that smashes through my body as I shout out my release. Gerald comes seconds later and I can feel him fill my ass.

As my body trembles and comes down off the high, I'm so aware of everything. The pain as Gerald takes himself out of me. The burn of my scalp to the humiliation that scorches my body. The man under me shifts and he removes himself from me. The heat of both bodies leaves and my hands shake as I push my bra back into place and try to button up my shirt. Tears soak my blindfold as I cry silently. What is wrong with me? How could I have enjoyed that? I feel so cheap. I can hear them get dressed, the door to the room opens and closes and I stay still, wondering if I am alone. Hands touch my shoulders and I jerk.

"It's okay." Gerald's voice has me shifting towards it.

"Sit on the edge of the bed." He commands and I do.

He's gentle as he pushes my underwear and trousers back on as far as he can. Taking my hands, he helps me stand and pulls them up the rest of the way. A sob shakes my shoulders as Gerald buttons me up. No more words are spoken as I'm led back to my room. I sense him as he pauses at the door, but he finally leaves.

I don't move, but stay standing in my room where he left me. I can't take off the blind fold. I'll hate what I'll see in the mirror. I feel so disgusted with myself. I don't recognize myself anymore. What is this place doing to me? What is *he* doing to me?

I still can't seem to meet my eyes in the mirror. "Are you okay? You seem pretty quiet today."

I smile at Candy in the mirror. "I'm fine." Linda is behind me and catches my eye.

"Okay everyone onto the floor." She claps her hands and everyone grabs last minute items before leaving, but I don't. Once the room is empty, I turn to Linda. She hasn't left either so she's expecting this.

"Taking control didn't work. I said no and it made no difference."

Linda smirks at me and my blood boils.

"What's so funny?" My anger burns my chest and I clench my fists.

"You don't say no to him." Her smirk is gone now.

"But you said to take control." My cheeks burn. I should have never listened to her.

"Yes, Cara, take control, but you're still in a box. You just have a choice of what you do while you're there. Do you understand?" She says stepping closer to me.

"No, I don't," I answer honestly.

"When I say take control I don't mean to say no, it's not an option. I mean you control the situation that is already transpiring."

"You think I should instigate it?"

"Whatever it takes to survive." Linda replies and something in her eyes has deepened.

"Did he do this to you too?" I hate the twist of jealousy that tightens in my stomach. Linda is gorgeous and I am no match for her.

"No. Now get out on the floor." She doesn't wait, but leaves the changing room, and I do as I'm told and go out onto the floor. Candy winks at me and I manage to give her a real smile back.

Can I instigate sex with him? Excitement burns my body as I spin around the pole. Doubts cloud my mind, Linda could be telling me what he wants her to tell me. I have no idea if she is playing me. Maybe at night they lay in bed together and laugh at naïve, messed up Cara. I swing faster trying to get away from my thoughts. I watch the floor. Wendy has her back to me as she raises a glass to her lips. The liquid is clear as she places the glass on the table beside her, but when she looks at me, I can see the alcohol in her eyes. Her nose flares as she stares at me before picking up the glass and draining it. Placing it on the table, she walks around the room, her eyes shooting to me to see if I'm still watching her. This place can do that to a girl. I understand how it can break you—or make you break yourself. Drink, drugs or to actually enjoy the sex, it's better than fighting it all. Fighting it isn't going to save any of us. I think in a place like this, we are all doomed to becoming so stretched and worn out, that we just dissolve like a tablet in water.

With my morbid thoughts, I dance until Linda comes for me to take me back to my room.

"How do I know you're telling me the truth?" I question.

"You don't." Linda doesn't flinch or even glance at me.

"Great. Thanks for everything."

Linda's hand tightens around my forearm as she stops me. Her brows furrowed. "I haven't done one thing to you. I owe you nothing. You being here is your own fault. Or your father's fault, but it has nothing to do with me. You understand?" Her anger has her lips thinning out into a straight line.

"You are the one who collects me and drops me off in my room. You are the one who knows what's happening to me. You are more responsible than he is." Her eyes flash a warning as she tightens her hold on my arm and pulls me the rest of the way back to my room. When she opens my room door, it's dark inside. She flicks on the light switch but no lights come on.

"He's here," I say to the darkness.

"Leave her." Gerald's voice comes from inside the darkened room. I think I feel Linda hesitate before she pushes me in and closes the door.

CHAPTER FOURTEEN

HER

I swallow the saliva that's gathered in my mouth the moment the door closes. *I'm going to take control.* I startle as hands push my hair back behind my ears, and material touches my face. A blind fold. I reach up to stop him.

"Leave it on," his voice is soft but deep as he holds the material against my face. It would be easy to follow directions. My body hummed with the thoughts of what happened the last time I put the blindfold on. In the darkness where all I had to do was feel. It is an easy pass, but one day it won't be so easy. Maybe one day I won't be enough.

"No." My hands tremble as I take the black material away from my face. I don't think but place it over his eyes, he doesn't stop me as I reach up on the tip of my toes and tie the blindfold at the back of his head. The smell of his cologne has my stomach tightening. It will be a smell I will never forget—with it comes a form of pain and so much pleasure. Warmth floods my body as I return to my feet. Power courses through my veins as he stands in front of me and waits. I'm not sure how to proceed.

"Sit on the bed." My voice sounds rocky and I start to question myself. His movements have me pushing the doubt aside as I find my way to the bed and touch the top of his head. I allow my fingers to sink in before descending to my knees. Saliva pools in my mouth and moisture gathers between my legs. Pushing down his jacket, he helps me but doesn't speak. I wish I could see him. Licking my lips I start to unbutton his shirt until I have it open. His skin is warm as my hands roam across his wide chest. Muscles tighten and twitch under my touch. The tremble in my hands grow as I reach his trousers and open the belt and zipper, before slipping my hand in. He groans the moment I touch him and lies back on the bed. I rise higher as I continue to stroke him. I've no idea what I'm doing, but from his heavy breathing, I'm doing something right. My core tightens and twitches, my nipples grow hard as they push against my shirt and I tighten my hold on him.

"Take off your trousers." I need more access. I'm not sure if I'm impressed or terrified when he does as I command. Sitting back on the bed, my hands roam his naked body as his large hands sink into my hair, his fingers tighten on the strands and he pulls. Pain burns my scalp and I try to pull away, but the pain only gets worse. I hiss and stop fighting it, my mouth brushes his meaty cock and he pushes my head down on it. I open my mouth and take all of it. Moving my mouth up and down, his hold on my hair loosens as he groans. When I pause, his fist grips my hair again and he forces my mouth down, I am losing control of the situation; he is gaining it back. I need to make the rules here, not him. My hand leaves his thigh and touches his balls as I take him deeper into my mouth. He loosens his hold as I continue to suck and lick, making my way slowly to the outside of his shaft. My other hand pushes his chest like he had done to me before and he lies back, releasing my hair. I don't linger, but instead, stand up and remove all my clothes. I am really going to do this. I touch his knees and feel him tighten under my palms. Dragging my hands up his legs, I climb on top of him. Looking down, I can only make out his outline but I bend down until my lips are touching his ear. His erection jerks against my stomach and all my nerve's spark.

"I'm going to remove the blindfold, but keep your eyes closed."

He raises his head slightly, giving me access to remove it. My fingers trail across his closed eyes, down his strong jawline, and to his chest. Lifting myself, I reach back and place his cock at my opening. I push down letting it dip inside me, we both groan but I don't go any deeper. I want to, but I also want to see how much control I can gain from this. I push my chest against him, my nipples hardening as they rub against his solid chest.

"Give me your hands." I hold the blind fold and when I touch his joined large hands in front of me, I bind them. "Keep them behind your head." They vanish and I sit back pushing down on his cock, it widens me, and I push down a bit more and don't stop until he fills me. I feel like I'll snap, he's so big, but I take all of him as I move back up and find a rhythm. My fingers flutter across my clitoris and I groan with pleasure. I push up and release him from me before moving beside him on the bed. I lick my own excitement off him and he juts his cock out, pushing it deeper into my mouth, I allow him this small movement as I lick and suck, each time he moans or groans it causes more wetness to pool between my legs. I want him back inside me, but I also want to see how long he will lie still for me. A salty taste enters my mouth.

"Cara, I'm going to come." His words are hoarse and I stop licking. He moves.

"Stay where you are." His hands grip my arm and I find myself on my back. He removed the binds.

"I can't." Rough hands touch my thighs as he spreads them apart. His cock is at my entry. I slam my legs closed stopping him and he pushes them open again. I am losing control. Panic starts to grow inside me and I rise quickly and shove his chest with a lot of force.

"Lie down."

He growls but does as I say. I know I don't have much time with him so I climb on top, not wanting to lose this bit of power. I rise and fall slowly, but my own need starts to grow. Gerald's large hands grip my ass as he helps me move up and down, the force of his hands spread my cheeks apart too.

"Faster." His growl has my core tightening and I move faster, slamming myself down on top of him before rising again. Sweat drips between my bare breasts and I move faster, my own pleasure heightening. Gerald releases my ass, but it doesn't break my rhythm as I move faster. His fingers tighten around my hard nipples and with sparks turning to flames inside me, I'm going to come. He's pounding into me, the sound of our flesh slapping together along with our mingled breaths has me coming all over his cock, crying out my release. His hands take my hips where he moves me up and down on his cock until he comes inside me, his warm liquid filling me.

I don't move as I fight for air. Sweat makes a pathway down my spine. He starts to stir under me and I'm ready to move but he sits up and holds my arms keeping me in place. His breath mingles with mine and once again I wish I could see him. There is now a familiarity in his touch and that causes a lump in my throat. His hands roam up and down my arms leaving goose bumps in its wake.

"Tell me your name." I lick my dry lips as I speak.

"Why?" His question brushes my face and I close my eyes.

There is power in knowing someone's name, or maybe I just want to know who I'm sleeping with. Who bought me? Who is still inside me? Is this Gerald? Is he the one who hurt Wendy? His name would give me something.

"I'm just curious." I settle on.

His hands leave my arms and go to my hips. I can sense his hesitation, but he withdraws from me and moves me aside before getting off the bed. Pulling my knees to my chest, I focus on the rustle of clothes as he gets dressed. I want to demand his name now. I feel like I'm losing control. Having it even for a short while makes the situation feel different and I want that feeling back.

"My name is Cara." I swallow and draw my brows down after saying it. I didn't think saying my name would feel this way. But it does. I don't feel like *Cara* anymore. Cara, who took care of her drunk father, who went to work every day to pay the bills. Cara, who reads and loved castles. Cara, the virgin.

"I already know your name." His response irritates me.

"I know, but now I'm giving that information up freely." Not because you bought me, I want to add, but don't push it.

There is silence and I sit in it for so long I think he might be gone, movement to the left of the bed has my gaze flickering there.

"My name is Gerald."

I can't stop the smile that grows across my face. I know he can't see me, but it's such a small victory. Biting my lip, I search the darkness again but he doesn't move or say anymore and I wonder again if he's still here. A soft click comes to my right and I stare at it.

"Gerald?" I question, pulling the quilt around my naked body before stepping out of the bed. The room is flooded in light and I close my eyes before slowly opening them and letting them adjust to the harshness of the light.

The room is empty. He's gone.

***

The next day in the club, I dance with a renewed energy. Last night I slept well for the first time in forever.

"Girl, how many coffees have you had?" Candy asks the moment I come down off the stage. I grin. "I don't drink coffee."

"Blasphemy." I continue to smile at her pretend outrage. "You seem ... different," she says looking at me from the corner of her eye.

"I'm just starting to get used to this." I shrug, hating the guilt and uncertainty that swirls in my stomach.

We walk together into the changing room. B is out back with Wendy. Thankfully, today they aren't fighting.

When Wendy sees Candy, she clicks her fingers while smiling. "What was the girl's name who had the false teeth?"

Wendy grins and I sit down in one of the chairs, twirling to face the mirror.

"Claire," Wendy says before Candy can think. They all burst out laughing and I turn in the chair to face them.

I'm surprised when Wendy fills me in. "Claire danced with us for like a week. But one of the days we were all in the back just talking and having a joke. I can't even remember what about."

"I do. It was your cat," B says pointing a long pink nail at Wendy.

"Don't start about my cat again." Wendy doesn't sound mad, but she rolls her eyes.

"Anyway she was laughing so hard she bent over and her false teeth popped right out of her mouth and slid across the floor." Wendy laughs and it's a nice sound. I find myself smiling at them.

"We all just went silent. I was like what the actual fuck." B chimes in.

Candy starts to roar laughing. "I never would have thought she had false teeth. I mean, she was pretty. But, that wasn't the worst part."

Now they are all laughing at the memory, I soak up their laughter.

"The dirty bitch walked right up to her own teeth and put them back in her mouth."

Their laughter becomes infectious and I can't stop the laughter that bubbles up to my throat.

"She hardly walked up to someone else's teeth and put them in her mouth. Unless there is something you want to tell us." Wendy fires back at Candy.

Candy makes her teeth more prominent and everyone laughs again.

"I think I actually threw up a bit in my mouth that day," B says wiping tears from the corner of her eyes. "She was rotten." The laughter dies down to giggles.

"So what was the story about the cat?" I ask and Candy winks at me.

"There is nothing wrong with my pussy." Wendy faces the mirror with a twinkle in her eye, knowing she opened the door to a different topic. The girls joke and laugh about Wendy's privates and it's nice just to sit and listen. Everything dies down as Linda arrives and we slowly trickle out onto the floor. I can sense her staring at me, but I don't look up. I don't want my good mood to flee. This is the best I have felt since coming to this place. Actually, this is the best I've felt in a very long time.

I haven't danced on the center stage yet, I'm still practicing on one of the smaller stages. I know I have only a short time left before I'll be returned to my room. It's always fairly dead when I arrive. I'm starting to wonder what this place must be like when it's filled with people. Taking the pole in my hand, I start to dance. It's not sexy, I'm just swinging around the pole, having fun. As I move around the pole, I count five men in total. Most of them sitting back in their chairs, either being served drinks or watching Wendy who steps onto the main stage. She's powerful in how she moves. I've never seen anyone move like her. It's such a shame that it has taken her to such a dark place.

CHAPTER FIFTEEN

HIM

My skin feels tight across my bones. I remove my jacket and place it on the back of the chair.

"Are you okay?"

I try not to react to Linda's sudden appearance, but honestly, I hadn't even heard her come into the library. I was so caught up in my own discomfort that I didn't hear her.

"Yes. Why?" I sit back in the chair and attempt to look relaxed, but I don't think I succeed.

"I knocked, but you didn't answer. You look like you've a lot on your mind."

"Thanks for the concern but I'm fine." I clear my throat as I open my laptop. "Is that all?" I don't look up at her and the click of her heels on the wooden floor has me glancing up as she leaves. The moment the door closes, I push down the flap of my laptop.

"My name is Cara." I have no idea why she told me her name, or why it was bothering me so much. I don't know why I told her my name. Scratching my neck doesn't stop the itch that burns under my skin. I pull off my tie and throw it on the desk. I need to get my head back in the game. My phone rings. Anger laces through my veins as Jake's name flashes across the screen. I hang up and throw the phone on the desk.

"My name is Cara." Her voice is spinning around in my head. I shouldn't have allowed her to blindfold me, but no one has ever done that to me. I have never felt that way when someone touched me.

Jake's name lights up the screen again, and this time I answer the phone.

"What do you want Jake?" I'm not in the mood for him. He probably wants money, or he's just trying to wriggle his way back in.

"I need your help."

"You have something that belongs to me," I say. I want Mickey's body back.

"Yeah I promise I will. But, I need you to come to the forest."

I'm sitting up and he has my attention. There is something in his voice that has a fist tightening around my chest. A long time ago, he had asked me to come to the forest too. I had to help him bury my grandfather's great Dane, that he had shot by accident. I often wondered if he was telling me the truth.

"I'm on my way." I'm ready to hang up.

"Thanks, Gerald."

I curse him, knowing whatever I'm walking into isn't good. I try not to let my mind conjure up crazy thoughts as I pull on my jacket and put my phone in my pocket.

I kneel down as I stare at Ger before running my hands across my face. Rising, I look to Jake for some reasonable explanation as to why Ger is dead. He's told me twice that he can explain, but I haven't heard his explanation yet.

"I'm waiting."

Jake wipes his nose and some of the blood that's splattered on his face spreads further. Removing a white napkin from the inside of my jacket, I step around Ger and hand it to Jake.

"I thought I told you to leave."

Jake takes the napkin, but doesn't wipe his face. "I did. I mean I was just searching the forest one last time."

"It's always one last time with you." I glance at Ger. From this angle I can see the right side of her head is bashed in. Scanning the forest floor, I can't see a weapon, and Jake isn't holding anything.

"I didn't think anyone would be here. You have tape up everywhere for people to keep out. So I thought I would take a look."

"And what, she appeared in the forest?" I say.

"Yeah she did. She was fucking waiting for me. She started screaming..." He trails off and points at her body.

"So you killed her?"

"You killed Mickey because you didn't like what he wore." His remark has me clenching my fists.

Jake starts to clean the blood off his face.

"Where's Mickey's body?"

He stops wiping himself and looks at me. I can see a smile in his eyes. "Help me get rid of her first and then I'll tell you."

"Killing you would be easier. You do know that." I didn't bring my gun, but if I had, I can't promise I wouldn't be burying two bodies instead of one.

"You wouldn't do that. I know you."

No, you don't. He has no idea of my capabilities.

"Tell me where Mickey's body is and I'll help you with this mess." I point at Ger, her head still seeping blood.

It's broad daylight. I glance around the forest, feeling aware of our surroundings now. Hopefully the tape keeps everyone else out.

"Fine. I buried him over here." He doesn't move.

"I want to see."

Jake hesitates but eventually he walks a few paces away from where Mickey had been originally buried.

"The grave looks too small," I say kicking leaves and twigs off a small patch of ground.

"Yeah, I was too tired to dig a large one."

I glare at Jake.

He grins. "So I cut him up."

"What did you use?"

"Don't worry. I disposed of it."

I take a step towards Jake. "How?" This isn't happening. He's a liability.

"I threw the chainsaw in the river."

"Stop talking," I say. All I want to do right now is kill him, and I don't have a gun.

"What did you use to kill her?"

Jake walks back to Ger's body and passes it, moving behind a tree. He reappears with a golf club.

"Why did you have that?"

"Protection. It's a good thing I had it too." The end of it is smothered in blood as he swings it up until it rests on his shoulder. The smile is back in his eyes and I'm beginning to think that I've underestimated Jake.

We bury Ger not far from Mickey. Now I have two bodies I need to move. Jake hasn't released the golf club, maybe he senses that I want it so I can kill him. I don't see any other way out of this.

"I'll get rid of this." Jake holds up the golf club to me.

I nod. "Don't forget to burn your clothes."

"Thanks, man." He grins at me as he walks backwards. "You're my alibi if this all goes south?"

"Sure," I lie and he turns around and jogs out of the forest. I don't leave as I look at the fresh clay and wonder what I've gotten myself in for. Taking my phone out of my pocket, I ring Linda and start walking back towards the castle. After ringing her three times and getting no answer, I start to worry. I dial the club, and Simon answers.

"Is Linda there?" I ask as I enter my private quarters. I love this suit, and now I have to burn it.

"No, she left earlier and she hasn't returned." Linda had never missed a day of work. I hang up and strip before getting into the shower. Why would Linda not be at work? She had come earlier to the library but she hadn't said what had brought her there.

Getting out, I dry off and re-dress in a fresh black suit. I left the other one in the fireplace. Lighting a match, I throw it in on top of it and watch my clothes burn. Dialing Linda again proves unfruitful. Something is wrong.

I make my way to the club and make sure I keep to the back of it. Cara isn't on the floor, but she'll be in the club today. I check Linda's office, it's unlocked. Everything is in perfect order. Stepping around her desk, I check a notepad that's open on her desk. It's a list of club duties. Sitting in her chair I pull out the first drawer, nothing only stationary is in it. I ring her mobile again, putting it on loudspeaker as I continue to search her desk. The phone rings out and goes to voicemail.

"Linda, it's Gerald. Where are you?" Hanging up, I sit back in the chair and look around the office. There's nothing here that can tell me where she is. Linda never put up a picture. Why would she? She didn't have anyone. I don't think she ever will. I don't think either of us will ever have the normal type of life that deep down we both craved.

I'd met Linda a year after I found Jake. Her father wasn't around and her mother never cared. Linda wasn't the most open person. So, when I'd found her bleeding and crying down an alleyway, she'd fought me. But I recognized her type of pain when I saw it. She'd been passed from one man to another and after years she had fought back. The result was her being left to die in an alleyway. She always reminded me of a feral dog. She wanted someone to take care of her but she made it so hard. Getting out of her office chair, I take one final look around her office before I return to the club. I sink further into the darkened corners. Cara's on stage and my whole body comes alive watching her. She curls her body around the pole and I want her on top of me, just like last night.

"My name is Cara." Her words echo in my ear. My eyes skim the room and I see two men watching her. My skin feels tight again and I pull at my shirt. I need to leave. Outside, I call Linda again.

"Answer your phone," I bark, while hoping that Linda gets the voicemail. I enter the house but don't go to my quarters. Sometimes Linda spends her time in the tea rooms, organizing parties. The moment I step in, I regret it. Mary waves at me eagerly. She must have been waiting for Linda. Another table of women watch me. I'm ready to leave, but Mary is out of her seat. I meet her halfway across the floor.

"We can't seem to find Lady Linda."

"She's out sick," I say to Mary.

Mary's eyebrows rise. "She really should have informed us. Me and the girls are waiting to discuss a very important party."

Every party—to Mary—is important.

"She should be back to work tomorrow."

"But we are already here." She points at the group of women who watch us. When I look at them, they wave and smile.

"I do apologize, Mary. But I have to return to work."

She pulls her chin into her chest and leans back while narrowing her eyes. "Why do I feel like I'm being dismissed?"

Because you are.

"Absolutely not. I do apologize and I'm sure Lady Linda will compensate you."

"She has a lot of compensating to do for me. She's really letting things slip."

I nod. "I apologize once again." I turn and leave before she can continue talking.

I leave the house and get my car from the garage.

"Simon, I found Linda, and she's sick."

"Ah, no. Hope she gets better soon." Simon's tone doesn't suggest any such thing and I wonder if he has anything to do with her disappearance. I rule it out. He's just a bartender.

"Yes, me too. But in the meantime. You're in charge." I slide into the car and switch on the engine. "Tell Candy she is to oversee things with the girls and you keep an eye overall. Ring me if you have any problems."

"No problem. I will run this ship tightly."

"Don't run away with yourself, Simon. It's a few hours." I reverse out of the garage and hang up on Simon. I ring Linda four more times as I drive to her house. She lives on the outskirts of Slane. She shares a small bungalow with another girl. I've never been inside her home, but I often drop her off at home after work. I don't see her car as I pull up.

I ring the doorbell three times before her roommate answers.

"Hi..." The brunette who answers the door smiles at me. "Mr. Norris," she says.

I have no idea what her name is. "I'm looking for Linda."

Her smile slowly dissolves. "Linda doesn't live here. She hasn't in months." Her brows pull down in confusion. "Is she okay? I thought she moved in with you."

I force a smile. "She's great and yes she did move in with me, but she left her phone at home and I was worried."

Her roommate's smile is back. "I always said that to her, you're one of the good guys."

I smile. *What the hell is Linda playing at?*

"I'm sorry I couldn't be more helpful."

"If she drops by just tell her I'm looking for her," I say stepping off the front porch.

"I will, Mr. Norris."

I get back into the car and ring Linda again. "I was just at your house. The one you don't live in anymore. You have a lot of explaining to do." I hang up and wave at her ex-roommate who's still at the door smiling at me.

CHAPTER SIXTEEN

HER

"I've been asked to escort you back to your room." There is an awkwardness in Simon's voice. He rocks on his feet while stuffing his hands in his black jean pockets.

"By who?" I fold my arms over my chest. I haven't seen Linda all day, and I wonder if something has happened. "Linda?" I quiz.

Simon flicks his head, moving his hair out of his brown eyes. "Yes, Linda." Simon sounds unsure, but I just nod.

What does it matter? "Okay. I'm ready."

He narrows his eyes at my outfit. "You're going outside in that?"

I had never been outside. Linda took me through back doors and hidden halls. "No. I'll show you."

Once we leave the club, my hearing takes some time to adjust. "This way." I open a door to the left of a coat rack. You would never have known a door existed as it's covered in the same wallpaper that's on the walls.

"This is cool." Simon's comment confirms my suspicions. That these hallways are only used by Linda.

"It must have been used by servants," I say as I keep my arms folded over my chest. Being down here with Simon makes me feel uneasy. I've never really thought of my surroundings before—with Linda. I never felt unsafe. The light only casts a dim shadow along the wooden hallway. Once we reach the door at the end, we step out into a much brighter hall.

"Down this way." I point to the end of the hall.

"You live here?" Simon looks at me with bright eyes and glances back at the hallway, with its large frames and stunning finishes.

"Kind of." I wouldn't say live here, but I don't know Simon, so I'm not going to divulge what I'm doing here. We reach my room and my stomach tightens as I twist the handle. When I turn, Simon is right behind me trying to get a look into my room.

"This is me," I say.

He glances at me. "See you tomorrow."

I give a tight smile before closing the door. I count to twenty with a pounding heart. I haven't released the door knob and I turn it slowly and pull, but the door doesn't open. I don't think Simon locked me in. The door must automatically lock itself.

I step into my room and start to take off my *work clothes*. The lights go out, and my heart does a dance that I am starting to associate with the arrival of Gerald. I turn to the bedroom door, hoping to see him when he enters. I wait for what feels like an eternity.

"Hello." His husky voice comes from behind me. Has he been in my room the whole time? Is that weird? This whole situation is weird.

"How did you get into my room?" I ask, turning around and facing more darkness.

"The same way I come into your room every time."

Now that I think about it, I never recall him coming in through the bedroom door. I've always been too afraid to notice things like that.

"What do you want?" My body is already humming with the idea of his hands on me, his cock inside me.

I tighten my thighs as I hear him remove his clothes. I want to remove mine too, but I'm not brave enough. There is a small voice in my mind telling me not to allow this to happen, that this is wrong. But in the disguise of the darkened room, I'm going to pretend that I asked him to come to my room. His large hands touch my shoulders and slowly make a burning path down my arms, pulling the straps of my suit with it. I don't stop him as he removes my clothes. The part that Linda said about taking control rises inside me. I need to take control or I'm not sure what will happen. My hands touch his solid chest and it reminds me how big he is. How strong he is, how much stronger than me he is.

I let my hands roam down and he stops me. "Hit me."

"What?" My voice shakes.

"I said hit me," his words brush my face and I take a step back.

"No."

He moves quickly, his hands sinking into my hair. "I said hit me. If you don't..."

I strike out and hit his chest and he releases my hair. My body temperature rises and I'm all too aware that I'm naked.

"Harder," his voice is rough and anger laces through it.

I want to say no, I don't want to hit him, but his silent threat that he didn't finish lingers in the room.

My hand's slap against his chest and the noise of skin hitting skin has me wanting to apologize.

"If you don't hit me," his voice rises.

My body reacts. My hand connects with his face, no doubt leaving a mark. His large hands are on me, pushing me, and I can't see. Each time I stumble he catches me. I swing and connect with his shoulder. My back hits the wall and he spins me around so I'm facing it, his body smashing up behind me.

"Try to hit me now." His harsh words brush my ear, but he has me pinned. I can't move. His knee pushes my legs apart and he maneuvers himself until I can feel his large erection at my opening.

"Let me go now." Panic claws at my throat as his body keeps me pinned.

He removes his cock and I think it's all over before he slips two fingers inside me. "You don't want me to let you go. You're turned on."

Am I? I have no idea what's happening to me.

His fingers rub against my lips, my tongue flicks out on reflex and I taste myself. "You taste that?" He pushes me painfully against the wall and I struggle for a moment.

"Yes," I shout angrily and he laughs in my ear. It isn't a nice laugh. His knee jerks my legs again, making me spread them further. He maneuvers himself once again at my opening. The tip enters easily and I feel such a sense of betrayal.

"Your pussy wants me."

I want nothing more than to push him away. He enters me fully now, and I gasp as he pulls out and starts to slam into me. This time is different from all the others. There is a savagery in his movements. My pleasure mingles with pain, but pain—this time—takes over as I tighten my eyes and wait for it to end. It does quickly, and only with his release. His sweat trickles onto my back.

"You'll soon learn to do as you're told." He takes himself out of me gently. It's such a contradiction to his words.

"You must feel so powerful, Gerald." I don't move even as he releases me from the wall. I stay against the wall as tears trickle down my face.

He doesn't answer, and I hate the silence now.

"Do you get off on hurting people?" I ask the darkness. He won't answer, but he is still here.

"What? Did someone hurt you?" I want to understand this madness. I have no sympathy for him, but I don't think one human being can be so cruel to another without a reason.

He still won't answer, and I push away from the wall as salty tears enter my mouth. "Why won't you answer me?" I feel drained now and the fight leaves me, the pain between my legs returns.

"You like when I take you," his words come from the darkness, but they are enough to start a fire in me.

"Fuck you."

His laughter startles me. It's loud and fills the room.

"So full of anger." I can still hear the laughter in his voice.

"You took me... and made me..." I trail off, my stomach twisting painfully.

"Your father gave you to me and I made you do nothing. Your anger has nothing to do with me."

The burn is immediate to the back of my throat and eyes. "I want to go," I finally say as tears drip off my chin.

"What about your father?" He's closer now. Yet, I didn't heard him move.

"Should I really care if you kill him or not?" I'm not sure who I'm asking the question to.

"Do you want me to kill him?" His question sounds so serious that it makes me really consider it.

My father sold me to this man who took my virginity, who has me pole dancing, and locked in a room. Anger bubbles in my stomach and burns the back of my throat like acid.

"No," I whisper while I slowly slide down the wall and sit on the ground. I didn't want my father dead, and right now I felt the damage was really and truly done to me. I didn't recognize myself anymore. This person who enjoyed sex with people she couldn't see. I participated in so much. I tell myself it's to stay sane, if I face the reality I won't last long here. I need to survive, and Linda said control is how I'll do just that.

"Where's Linda? Have you hurt her?" I ask from the ground while pulling my knees into my chest.

He exhales loudly and I'm starting to wonder why he is still here.

"No, I didn't hurt her. Did your father hurt you?"

His question once again startles me. He seems to be doing that a lot tonight. "Like the way you do?"

I can hear him moving, I'm searching the darkness. "Why won't you let me see you?" I ask, but I know he won't answer me.

"Does your father put his hands on you?"

It's my turn to laugh now. "You sound angry, Gerald." He did, which pissed me right off. "Like someone might have played with your toy." I'm shouting again. I feel like I'm losing my mind.

"I am. You're mine." He must be right in front of me. So close. His words confuse me. He sounds almost like he's fond of me.

"Leave me alone," I tell the darkness. I sit for a while and I can hear his movements before something clicks and I know that I'm alone well before the lights come on.

I'm left alone until the next night. I'm walking a path in front of my bed when the door opens. The relief I feel at seeing Linda isn't normal. She looks a mess, but she's alive. She just looks like she had a wild night.

"Are you ready?" She won't meet my eyes and I pause.

"Are you okay?"

"Yes. Are you ready?" She sounds pissed and I'm sick of being locked in this room, so I follow her out the door. She doesn't speak but I feel her watching me, which is odd. Each time I glance at her, she looks away. Once we reach the club, I pause at the door.

"Are you okay?" I know we weren't friends, but I can feel how distressed she is.

Her head snaps up to me and her eyes shimmer. Seeing her display such emotion has fear crawling across my skin.

"No. Something, there's something I need to tell you."

I'm holding my breath, and I can't even begin to think what she wants to tell me.

"Is this why you weren't here yesterday?" I ask, taking a step towards her.

She exhales loudly and her phone rings. Taking it out of her pocket she stares at the caller ID, then at the door of the club before she answers.

"I'll be in… what?" Linda takes the phone away from her face and opens the club door.

"What's wrong?" I ask, but she doesn't answer me. I follow her to the changing rooms. I can hear the chaos before we enter.

"She isn't breathing." Candy's on her knees leaning over Wendy whose body is still, too still. Linda doesn't hesitate but moves beside Candy and places her head over Wendy's mouth. She checks her neck for a pulse.

I can't seem to react as Linda starts to do CPR on Wendy. Candy's cries are the only sound in the changing room as the rest of the girls, who I don't know, stand around and just wait.

"Cara." Linda doesn't turn around as she calls me, but I'm right beside her in seconds.

"I need you to take over compressing her chest when I tell you."

I want to say no.

I nod and when Linda breathes into Wendy's mouth, she looks at me. "Okay start."

I do. I keep the pumping motion going for as long as Linda tells me.

"Candy, go get Damien. Now."

Candy leaves and it feels like the circle of girls shuffles closer around us.

"Stop." Linda listens closely. Her smile of relief is instant. "She's breathing."

A few girls exhale a sob of relief too.

"What happened?" Damien, who I recognize from the oak doors, looks down at Wendy. He isn't overly alarmed. The more I stare at him, the more unsettled I feel. He seems so unaffected at seeing Wendy on the floor.

"I need to get her to a hospital. Shut the club down."

All the girls start chattering at once. I hear one ask *what about pay?* When my eyes clash with hers, she stands a bit taller. "I still got to eat." She defends her callous remark. She fades out as all the voices mesh together. It's seconds before the space is cleared out. Linda's gone with Wendy, and Candy follows too.

I enter the club. The lights are on, half glasses of alcohol sit on nearly every table. The place must have been packed. Damien steps back into the club as I wander through the empty space moving chairs back into place as I go. Simon is behind the bar, clearing glasses. When he notices my approach, he smiles.

"Can I get a vodka?" I ask Simon as I reach the bar and sit down.

"You sure?" he quizzes.

"Yeah. Work's over. So give me the Goddamn drink."

Sniggers sound behind me. I glance over my shoulder to see Damien grin as he sits beside me. He's a big guy, and I wasn't sure what to make of him. Any man who works here, and especially guards the door to the sick rooms out the back, isn't much of a *man* in my opinion.

"I know a girl just like you."

"What, a pole dancer?" I ask, as Simon places the drink in front of me. I knock the drink back.

Damien sniggers again. "No. Mouthy."

"I'm not normally like this," I say into the empty glass that's removed from my fingers. Simon, refills it and I give him a soft smile of thanks before I drink it all.

"What happened to Wendy?" I place the glass on the bar, but Simon doesn't refill it and I don't want to push my luck. I have no money to pay for the drinks.

"Two more Simon." Damien orders. "Drugs or drink. Who knows?" When Simon places the drinks on the counter, Damien slides one towards me.

"For the shock," he says while raising the glass to his lips.

"Yeah, for the shock," I repeat and I can't stop the sarcasm that enters my voice. I didn't think anything could shock me anymore after being in a place like this.

Damien shakes his head while he sniggers again. "Yep, just like her," he says before he downs his drink.

I don't ask who he thinks I'm like. I really don't care.

CHAPTER SEVENTEEN

HIM

After leaving Cara, I drank too much. It's something I gave up a long time ago, but she provoked something inside me. I sensed her excitement the moment I arrived in her room. I needed her to remember that I held the power, that I could hurt her. Leaving her crying told me I got my point across. I'm not sure why it's bothering me so much.

"My name is Cara." That moment when she had given me her name freely after everything I've done to her. It's slowly eating me alive.

Three quick knocks at the library door have me sitting up. Linda steps in. When she reappeared yesterday, I was too angry to speak to her. She gave me some lame excuse about being sick, then she took off for the club.

"How's Wendy?" I ask, hating that my club was shut down last night. It was overkill on Linda's part, but she still isn't herself so I am letting her poor judgment slide.

"Yeah, she'll be okay." Linda folds her arms across her chest. The white and black polka dot shirt is tucked into a high-waisted beige skirt.

"I want to ask you something." Linda looks shifty, nervous so I don't speak but just nod.

"Cara's father." Linda swallows and looks away, before glancing at me from the corner of her eye, like she's terrified of the answers.

"He's dead."

I don't react. I don't care. It changes nothing here.

"Was it you?" This is what's wrong with Linda? She thinks I killed Cara's father.

"No."

"Why don't I believe you?" Linda hasn't stepped any further into the room and for the first time, in a very long time, she is afraid. Afraid of me.

"Because, Linda, I'm telling the truth. Something you don't seem capable of."

Linda swallows. "What's that supposed to mean?"

I don't answer. I just sit back further in my chair and let her answer her own stupid question.

"Is this about where I live?"

It doesn't take long. "Yes. You lied about where you live."

She unfolds her arms. "No Gerald. I did live there. I just moved, and where I live is none of your business."

I hide the grin as I watch Linda unfold again from the fragile person she's becoming. As we stare at each other, I understand that she isn't going to tell me where she lives now, and frankly, it's fine. The fact that Linda is back is all that really matters.

"I better get back to the club."

"Is Cara in her room?"

She bristles again at the mention of Cara's name.

"Yes." I can sense her uneasiness.

"Did you tell her about her father?" I ask.

"Of course not." Linda swallows a lump of guilt.

"Good." I stare at her until she can't hold my eye any longer.

"I better get back."

I don't say anymore as she walks out of the room. Opening the drawer, I take out the two masks that I had placed there earlier and just hold them. Mary's swingers party has started and she has left an open invitation for me to come. Excitement courses through me as I think of Cara's body. She's beautiful. She's mine. My skin gets that tight feeling again and I cough to try to release it, but I still feel stretched. Taking both masks, I don't leave through the library door but through the hidden hallways. Pulling out the Jewish Bible halfway, the book shelf clicks and I pull it away from the wall. The lights immediately turn on. I close the door behind me as I take the same path I've been taking since Cara arrived. Once I reach the secret compartment to her room, I take out my phone and knock out the power to her room. Counting to ten, I push open the door and step inside. Closing the panel gently behind me, I try to let my eyes adjust to the darkness. I can hear her breathing. It's loud today. She's afraid. A part of me thinks it's good, while another hates that I've put the fear there. I follow her breathing. She's standing close to the bedroom door.

"Have you come to hurt me again?"

She sounds angry and afraid. "No." She inhales harshly at my closeness.

Reaching out, I touch her and push her hair back before placing the half mask on her face.

"A mask?" She quizzes.

I place my own on before taking her hand. She doesn't stop me as I twine her fingers with mine. I take her over to the panel in the wall and push it open. The pop is immediate and I step through bringing her with me. She glances around her as I close the panel behind us. Turning to her, her eyes roam my face. I forgot that this will be the first time she's seen some of me. The mask I wear only covers the top half of my face. The rise and fall of her chest is quick. Her pulse flickers along her neck. I stand and allow her to stare at my face. She looks so small in front of me. I tower over her and I wonder now what she sees. I shouldn't care, but for some reason I do. I take her hand and her eyes snap to mine. Her moss green ones are so wide, and I want to ask her what she's thinking. I also want her to keep looking at me the way she is, like she's in awe of me. I take a step closer and she doesn't step away. She tilts her head back so she can look up into my eyes. My own heart picks up and I'm not sure what's wrong with me. Turning away, I start to walk and she doesn't pull her hand out of mine as I move through the hallways with too much turmoil in my heart.

We step out into a large hallway. No one's around as I close the panel once Cara is beside me. "Where are we going?" she asks. I'm very aware how her hand still rests in mine. I'm also aware that I like it there, so I let it go.

Room number *Sixty Nine* takes up most of the top floor where we hold these kinds of very private parties. I open the door and step in. Cara follows, and I try to see this place through her eyes. The wide space we walk into holds only a large black round table. It's completely constructed from marble. You can't see over it as it holds a lot of different plants. A chandelier hangs above it, casting light in the large space. Under our feet, a red, lush carpet molds around all the bare feet that sink into it. People in only masks drink and mingle, some start early while others watch. I glance at Cara as she takes a step towards the door. Capturing her hand in mine, she stares at me with fear in her eyes. I leave the main area and step under the large white arches. The lighting in here is dimmer, the illusion of hundreds of candles burning is cast throughout the space. Large cushions, couches, and blankets are spread throughout the room. The end of the room is dominated by a large fireplace. The fire is lit and flickers shadows across the three women who are pleasuring each other in front of it.

I turn to Cara, who's taking everything in with a look of horror on her face. "Close your eyes," I tell her and wide green eyes flicker to mine. Her lashes flutter down as she does as I ask. Her face is perfection. Pale skin that hasn't a blemish on it, makes her lips always look a deep red. Cara's still in her outfit from the club, so I don't have much to remove, but I take my time pushing the straps down her arms, feeling her skin under my fingertips. Goosebumps rise in the wake of my touch. I step closer and inhale the smell of Cara. Lavender, and something sweet. I reach behind her and unclip her bra, letting it fall to the floor. Her breasts bounce free, her nipples already hard. She keeps her eyes closed and I dip my head, taking one of her nipples in my mouth. She hisses in pleasure and my trousers tighten. Brown eyes stare at me as I suck Cara's nipple. The girl appears behind Cara and runs her hands down her chest. I can feel Cara stiffen, but she doesn't open her eyes to see who has joined us. My mouth leaves her breast as I reach down and run my fingers under the band of her pants, she tenses under my touch but doesn't stop me as I slide her pants down her legs, she steps out of them easily and she looks glorious standing naked in front of me.

The woman moves around to the front of Cara, her hands dragging across her chest. I used the moment to remove my clothes, my trousers painfully tight. Once my trousers are off, my erection springs free. Brown eyes leave Cara and take me in, her eyes flicker greedily to my cock. She's moving to get down on her knees but I grab her wrist, stopping her. Moss green eyes that are alive bore into mine and she's all I want. I release the other woman and descend to my knees. Cara watches me as I place my hands on her hips and bury my head between her legs. Her hands instantly sink into my hair and she gasps. Using my tongue, I push her folds open and taste the sweetness that is Cara. It's hard to get access this way. Leaning out I stand and notice the other girl hasn't left, she's still touching Cara's chest and she follows us as I lead Cara to a huge cushion, laying her back on it. Spreading her legs, I don't hesitate as I place my head back between her legs. Her body rises and I push it back down as I sink my tongue deeper into her sweet pussy. Nails run down my spine before stopping at my ass. Irritation has me coming back up. This stupid girl isn't leaving. Reaching out, I take her face roughly and force her down onto my cock. She takes it, sucking. I glance at Cara who's watching and I swear she looks hurt. She has no right. So why do I feel guilty? I ignore the feeling and push my cock deeper down this woman's throat. Closing my eyes, I fling my head back and try to enjoy it. Fingers touch my lips.

"Taste me." Cara's kneeling up, her fingers on my lips and I suck them, tasting all that is sweet about her. Pulling myself from the woman's mouth I turn fully to Cara, my erection is almost painful. I need to be inside her sweet pussy. Bending her over, I spread her ass cheeks to give me more access to her. I don't hold back as I push my cock into her tightness. The woman wanders off and is soon replaced by a man who immediately reaches for Cara while I'm fucking her. He places his cock at her mouth and I watch as she takes it easily. I've slowed my pace, but now I start to pick back up as she takes this man's cock deeper into her mouth. The girl returns again and moves behind me, where she runs her hands across my ass before slowly touching it. Her long nail sinks in and I slow my pace on Cara to give the woman more access to me. Her finger disappears fully into my ass as I sink my cock deeper into Cara. The other man takes his shaft out of Cara's mouth and starts to masturbate. The finger leaves my ass and I start to pound into Cara who moans in pleasure. The other woman kneels down beside Cara and licks the top of the other man's cock. Her tongue flicks out and he quickens his pace, she crawls closer until she takes one of his balls in her mouth and sucks. I remove myself from Cara and flip her around, she looks up at me, her eyes buzzing like a woman who's drunk, she is drunk on lust. I push two fingers into her opening and remove them, the shine of her excitement coats my fingers. I crawl up to her and place them on her lips like she had done to me.

"Taste it." She does. Her small pink tongue flicks out and wraps around my fingers. She sucks them and I want her warm mouth around my cock. The man who had joined us releases his cock and moves towards Cara, and I don't like it as he bends his head and takes one of her breasts in his mouth. His lips trail up her neck and I want to kill him.

Taking Cara by the arms, I pull her up and away from them. She's dazed, and they don't look so happy. I take the same breast that the man just had and I suck it, removing his touch from her body. I want her so badly, but for the first time, I don't want to share her. I take her hand in mine and she doesn't object as I pull her up and walk us through the room. Near the fireplace, there is a panel that will take us out of here. I glance around to make sure no one is watching and push it open. Stepping through into a dimly lit old hallway, I wait until the panel clicks back into place before I push Cara up against the wall. Her eyes are still swimming with lust, but I see something else there, I'm not sure what. My heart pounds as I stare into moss green eyes. Pulling up one of her legs, I place my cock at her opening and slide it in. Her warmth and wetness wrap around me and I groan before grabbing her other leg, and pulling both up so they are wrapped around my waist giving me full access to her. I push in and she groans into my neck, her hot breath against my skin has me wanting to fill her with my cum. I pound harder, her breast's bouncing against my chest. She removes her head from my neck, her hands tightening on my shoulders as I pound into her. All I want to do is kiss her.

My eyes flicker to her red lips. It's one rule I don't break. I don't ever kiss anyone. I pound deeper, my balls slapping against her flesh.

"Harder." Her one word has me nearly losing it. I pound harder, faster. I'm so close and I can see so is she. I give in to every temptation I have and press my lips against hers. It's like she freezes for a second before her body responds to me like never before. Her tongue fills my mouth and I know I'm going to come.

CHAPTER EIGHTEEN

HER

My lungs seize as he pushes his lips against mine. I'm so aware of everywhere our bodies meet, but his lips against mine scorches my flesh. I don't think, but push my tongue into his mouth as I rise high on the wave as he pushes himself into me. My back slams against the wall and he doesn't slow down. I don't want him to. I'm so close to coming. My hands greedily touch as much of his flesh as I can. I can't seem to get close enough to him. I want more of him and when his teeth graze my swollen lips, I know I'm going to shatter. I call out as I come all over him. His own release is almost immediately after mine. The aftermath tremors have him jerking inside me. His lips are still pressed against mine as our breaths mingle together.

My heart pounds rapidly in my chest like I've run a mile. His skin glistens with sweat. He still holds me up, our bodies still joined and I'm not yet ready to have him step away. I know what happens after. I'll be taken to my room where I will be left alone with my thoughts, and right now my thoughts are going to dark places. The usual guilt is starting to swirl, but something else is rising to the surface.

Gerald slowly removes himself from me before allowing my feet to touch the ground. His mouth leaves mine, but as I stand, our bodies are still pressed against one another. I focus on his strong jaw and chin. Seeing half his face has done weird things to me. He is gorgeous. I am only seeing half his face, and now I wonder what seeing all of him would do to me. Blue eyes that start so dark on the outside, and seem to lighten until they mesh with his black irises consume me. I want to tell him I don't want to leave; I don't want to go back to my room. His hands are resting on my shoulders, my own pressed against his chest, his heart still races under my fingertips. My own heart is racing now for a completely different reason than it had before.

"Stay here," he tells me, and I'm startled at the sound of his voice after so much silence.

I nod and he steps away from me. I'm instantly cold and aware of how naked I am. Seeing Gerald in the light has me clenching my legs together. I'm surprised at how easily my body comes alive as I watch him move down the hall. My eyes drink him in, from his long muscular legs to his perfect ass that begs to be grabbed. His broad back is wider than I pictured in my head. Muscles shift as he walks. He disappears and I lean my head against the wall trying to make sense of what I am feeling.

It doesn't take him long to return. I'm disappointed when I see all his flesh is nearly covered up. Black trousers and a black t-shirt cover his body, but he's still amazing to look at. He hasn't removed the mask and I focus on the angles of his jawline as he hands me a silk black dressing gown that I wrap around my body. He's staring at me and I'm not sure what's happening.

"Can I remove my mask?" I ask. My skin is warm and flushed under it.

"Yes."

I remove it and am all too aware of how I must look. I'm not sure if I prefer the darkness of the room. In the darkness, I can pretend—but here in the light, seeing him...it's making this all *very* real.

I flicker a glance up at him to find him watching me. My heart starts to do a merry dance and I want it to calm down.

I want to ask what now, but I also don't want this to end.

"Are you thirsty?"

The question surprises me and I nod before speaking. "Yes."

He doesn't move immediately, it's like he knows I want to look at him and he is allowing it. I want the mask off, I want to see him, but another part of me doesn't. I break eye contact and he turns and I follow him. This place is a maze, we move through several small hallways, I would never remember my way around here.

"They don't tell you about these passageways during the tour," I say, allowing my hands to trail along the old green wallpaper. Gold shapes coat them and if you stare too much it makes you dizzy, so I focus on Gerald's wide back.

"It isn't public knowledge."

I smile at his back. It is weird hearing him speak. I have so many questions, but being out of my room and seeing something different keeps all my questions at bay.

Gerald stops and pushes a part of the wall. It clicks and I watch as it opens. We step into a library. Gerald closes the bookcase behind us before closing the main library door. My stomach lurches as he turns a key, locking us in. The high ceilings and the architecture of the room consume me as I move in a full circle, taking it all in. I hear the rattle of glasses, but I just want to touch everything. Taking three steps up, I stand on a carpeted space that's vacant of furniture. Bookshelves are built around me from ceiling to floor. I've been in this room before, but I was too afraid to really take it in. I turn to find Gerald watching me. He's standing near a Queen Ann chair that I remember him sitting on when he asked me to dance for him. My pulse jumps as he walks towards me.

"Do you live here?" I ask as he climbs the three steps and places the glass in my hand. I take a sip of the liquid that burns the back of my throat.

"Yes." His answer is quick and he glances around the space much like I had.

"Do you like to read?"

I take another sip before I answer. We're standing here like two normal people having a conversation, but there is nothing normal about this.

"Why do you wear the mask?" I step closer to him and he doesn't move.

"I ask the questions." He takes a drink from his glass and now I can't even pretend this is normal. He just reminded me of how wrong all of this is. But I don't want to go back to my room. My bare feet sink into the carpet as I walk to the bookshelves.

"Yes. I love to read." I glance at Gerald over my shoulder. He hasn't moved and my stomach quivers. I've never seen eyes like his. They hold so much coldness, and yet I see a spark of interest as he studies me.

"You can take some back to your room." His words should make me smile, but my body feels heavy. I don't want to go back to my room.

I take another sip of my drink. "Did you grow up here?" I ask as I stare at all the old books. I can tell from the covers that the English wouldn't be easy to read and wouldn't be to my taste. Taking a book off the shelf, I open it and enjoy the smell of the musty pages.

"Yes." His answers are always one worded, yet I felt like he is sharing, which is something I don't think he's used to.

"Were you happy?" I turn to him now, holding the book to my chest.

He blinks and takes a drink. "No."

"Did someone hurt you?"

His smile is quick, white teeth flashing. It only lasts a second and it's filled with pain but my stomach and heart jumps.

"Your hell bent that someone hurt me." He finishes his drink, the earlier pain gone. His eyes look bluer now, colder.

"I think we all act from an emotion we've felt. Some are stronger than others."

He grins and once again there is no humour, but I'm fascinated by his mouth. "Like lust?"

My face heats up immediately and his eyes shine. He knows he is steering us away from him. I tell myself to be strong.

"Yes. Or pain."

His eyes harden and he stares at me. "Finish your drink." He turns away from me and I regret pushing so hard. I empty the glass and walk to the bookshelf where I replace the book.

"You can take it with you."

I turn to him as I keep my hand on the book. "I don't want it."

A knock at the library door has me staring at it. Someone turns the knob. "Gerald." Linda's voice penetrates the door.

He looks unsure as he glances at me. "Stay there." He tells me as he makes his way to the door. I want to ask him where else would I go. He half opens the door.

"Is everything okay? Why are you wearing a mask?" I can hear Linda's inquisitive voice. Stepping away from the books I carefully take the three steps, I pause when my bare feet touch the hard wood.

"Yes. I'm busy." Gerald's voice is filled with irritation.

I take a few more steps until I can see Linda.

"I'll come back another time," she says before her brown eyes snap to me, they widen slightly in surprise and then she's gone as Gerald closes the door.

"I thought I told you to stay up there," he says while locking the door.

"Oh, I thought you meant as in this room." I had known exactly what he had meant. He turns and that smile that makes my toes curl but my heart pound in fear is back on his face.

"You knew exactly what I meant." He takes a step towards me and I take a step back.

"You were disappointed it was Linda, weren't you?" He steps closer and I continue to step back. "Were you going to scream for help?" The thought had never entered my mind. I hit a desk and my hands immediately grip the wood.

"Honestly, no."

He doesn't stop his advance until he's right in front of me. His knee nudges my legs apart and he steps in between them.

"I should punish you for lying to me."

Excitement bubbles up inside me. "But I didn't lie."

His hand moves to my hip and roams across the nightgown, he pulls the rope that holds it together. The air touches my skin as he opens it fully. His fingers trail across my thigh before he touches me. I gasp, wondering how the hell I could be ready for him again, but I am. His fingers dip inside me as he leans in, and whispers in my ear. "What should your punishment be?"

I bite my lip as his lips trail kisses along my cheek before they reach my mouth. I'm two seconds away from begging him to take me here and now on this desk. His fingers move deeper and another one enters my wet pussy. His kiss is hard and I meet it with my own want. Flicking my tongue into his mouth, his tongue enters mine and I moan and whimper as he removes his hand. I hear his zipper before his erection pushes against me. He doesn't put it in, instead he moves back.

"Bend over." I'm panting, feeling flushed, but I get off the desk and do as he asks. The dressing gown is still on me and covers my back. He removes it quickly and spreads my legs before placing his cock at my opening. He bends around me, his arms reaching for my breasts and squeezes my nipples. The pain has me hissing and he slams into me.

"You're so wet." His words have me clenching around him inside me, and he releases my breasts as he stands up straight. He's displaying that same savagery as he had in the bedroom when he had taken me against the wall. His flesh slaps against mine painfully, only this time I want him to go harder. I want more.

My hands grip the edge of the desk as he groans, sinking deeper into me—if that's even possible. I feel stretched, he's filling every inch of me, filling me up with all of him. His movements are frantic now as he pounds into me, and I'm so close to releasing all over him.

"Come for me, Cara." The use of my name sends me over the edge and I do as he asks. I come all over him as he releases himself inside me. I'm still panting as Gerald pulls out of me. I don't move as he zips himself back up. I glance at Gerald through my hair and I hate how I feel when I look at him.

How could anyone have the power to make me feel like this? I've never felt so alive, but also something inside me has died since I arrived here.

He holds out my nightgown and I turn, meeting his sharp blue eyes. My gaze flickers to his lips and I want to kiss them slowly. I want to really feel them on mine, but he steps away from me and walks up to the bookshelves.

"We better get you back to your room," he says while opening the bookcase.

"Yeah. My mother will be beside herself waiting on me." My angry words fall from my lips and I don't expect him to hear me, but he does and he laughs.

I'm frozen. It's not the cruel or cold laughter that I had heard before. He's smiling and I'm spinning, my heart pounds and heat fills my hands.

His smile slowly dissolves off his face as I stand frozen, staring at him. He has no idea the effect he has on me. How one action or reaction from him could send me into a spin. It's like my brain has short circuited and it takes me a moment to place one foot in front of the other until I reach him. I'm still high on Gerald, so when I pause I look up at him.

"You should smile more," I say.

"Maybe I will, Cara." The use of my name has a smile that I can't stop spreading across my face.

"You should smile more too."

"All I need is a reason, Gerald."

His eyes light up and I wonder—does me using his name have the same effect on him as it does on me?

He moves through the door and I follow him down the hallway that leads to my room. My cage, my loneliness and worst of all, my thoughts.

CHAPTER NINETEEN

HER

The club is busy when I arrive the next day. There are new girls here that I haven't met before. Candy introduces me, but the names go right over my head. I can't stop thinking about Gerald.

"Earth to Cara." Candy narrows her eyes at me but she's smiling. "What are you thinking about? Or should I say *who*?"

My face flames, but I'm not sure if Candy can see it through the layers of makeup that's on my face. Before I get to answer her, Linda steps into the changing room and scans the girls before she focuses on me.

"You're up," she says with a tilt of her head. She's been acting even stranger than normal, and I wonder if it's because she saw me in the library.

I knew I would eventually have to dance center stage, but still my stomach twists and tightens.

"You will kill it girl," Candy's words of encouragement have me smiling.

"Thanks."

I step up to Linda. "I'm ready," I say more to prepare myself.

She doesn't smile. There's a darkness in her eyes that I haven't seen before. "Good. I'll take you to the room."

Coldness seeps into me and I can't seem to move. "Room?"

"The back room. There's a client waiting for you." She smiles almost smugly at me, and so many thoughts rush through my mind.

"Does Gerald know?" Pain like I've never felt before burns through me.

She sniggers. "I own you, Cara. Once you're in this club. You're mine to do with as I see fit. Gerald knows." She adds, and it's like someone is twisting a knife. I follow Linda numbly as I glance around the club. I'm waiting for someone to say that Linda has made a mistake, but no one does. We reach the door and Damien steps aside, he doesn't even blink as his eyes collide with mine.

"Linda," I plead. She turns to me and places a finger over her lips. I want to beg her not to do this. I've allowed Gerald to use me so why not some other man? Why does this feel different? Linda stops at the last door and opens it.

"She's here." She smiles at whoever is inside. Each step feels like an eternity before I step up beside Linda and look in the door. A man who must be in his sixties sits on the bed. He's trim and he looks like your friend's dad. He looks normal.

"Hello dear." His voice is soft, his smile warm. I don't like it.

"Cara is here to do as you please." Linda informs him and nudges me in the back. I step deeper into the room.

"The Boom Boom Rooms are my favorite." His sly smile and childlike expression has me glancing at Linda. There is a moment of uncertainty as she forces another smile.

"I'm very glad to hear it. If you need assistance, there's a bell on the table."

A silver polished bell is the only thing sitting on the mahogany table in the corner. The room is dominated by the bed that the man is sitting on. The rest is just lighting.

"Hello Cara." His smile is sweet and my stomach lunges as Linda leaves. I want to cover myself, but I keep my hands hanging at my sides. Sweat starts to gather on his forehead as he stares at me.

"Did Linda tell you what I want?" He looks at me from under his lashes. Black hair that's split in the middle makes him look odd.

"No." Linda hadn't told me anything.

He bristles, not happy with having to explain. "I want you to masturbate for me. I want to watch you."

I have no desire to come. I thought this was for *his* pleasure, not mine.

I walk to the bed and he holds up his hands, stopping me. "Don't touch me. Lie on the floor. The bed is mine." I want to ask him what his deal is. Who comes here and doesn't want to be touched? Maybe I should count myself lucky. I lie on the floor and glance at him as he starts to remove his clothes. His laced shoes come off first and he places them perfectly together. I lie on the floor as he removes all his clothes and folds them, even down to his white pants.

"You may start," he says while removing a pillow case from a pillow.

I slip my hand between my legs and start to touch myself. I'm not going to come like this. I've never faked it before, but I'm sure I'll manage. I glance at him as he places the pillow case on the bed before he sits down. His eyes meet mine and he smiles.

"Could you remove your underwear so I can see?"

Gritting my teeth, I do as he asks.

"Spread your legs more."

Closing my eyes, I spread them as far as I can.

"Ah that's perfect."

I want to close my legs. I hate that this man has such access to me. I feel it would be easier if it was quick sex. I feel so exposed. It's degrading. I hold back the tears as I touch myself. His groans and grunts are loud. He's masturbating, his focus fixed between my legs. I close my eyes again, and this time I think of Gerald. I think of his hands on my body, his cock inside me and I start to grow wet. I dip my fingers inside myself and rub the juices all over my clitoris. A strong jaw and perfect lips I picture. I picture intense blue eyes watching now. It's Gerald watching me now. It's Gerald sitting on that bed. I groan in pleasure and I try to ignore the grunts that are coming from the bed. Grunts that Gerald would never make. Movement has me opening my eyes. He's standing now, his cock in his hands as he pumps it roughly. He moves until he's standing over me.

"Come for me, Cara."

I snap my eyes shut. I shouldn't have looked at him. My body is drying up. I quickly try to pull back the image of Gerald as I touch myself. I'm instantly wet as I dip my fingers back in and out quickly. My free hand slides to my breast and I squeeze my nipple. My body hums and I move my hand faster.

"Watch me. Like I'm watching you." I open my eyes. My vision fills with his balls as he pulls his cock with a speed I match. He's up here, but Gerald's down there. Fucking me. I release quickly all over my hands. Warm liquid splashes my chest and I close my eyes as his cum sprinkles across my face. I don't want to move from the ground. I just want a hole to appear under me and swallow me whole.

I open my eyes. "Do you have a towel?" I quiz. The man is back at the bed using the pillow case to clean himself with.

"Don't move." He sounds angry now. Once he has pulled on his white pants, he picks up the silver bell and rings it. I start to get up.

"I told you not to move Cara."

My blood boils at the use of my name. A soft knock sounds at the door before Linda enters. I die a little more as she glances down at me.

"You never informed Cara of what I wanted. I had to explain myself. It made me feel uncomfortable."

Uncomfortable. I'm lying here practically naked with cum all over me while they discussed how he felt uncomfortable.

"I do apologize, an oversight on my part. There will be no payment this time."

I want to ask for a towel again to clean him off me. But speaking will get their attention, and right now they are focused on payment.

"I feel Cara deserves something."

My skin burns.

"You can leave her a tip if that makes you more comfortable Carl."

"It would. Thank you, Linda."

The door closes and Carl continues to get dressed. I don't move. I don't even open my eyes.

"I've left a little something for you," he says and I look up at him as he steps over me. I don't move as he leaves the room. I need to get up. I need to move. The pillowcase he had used to clean himself with is on the floor. I crawl over to it and pick it up and clean my chest and my face.

It's okay, Cara.

I fix my clothes and stand up. Twenty euro sits on the wooden table. *Twenty euros.* That's what I'm worth. I'm staring at it when the door opens again.

"You are finished." Linda speaks from behind me and I clench my fists.

Anger heats my body up and I turn to her. "What, being degraded and humiliated?" I say, and I can feel the scorch of shame burn my chest.

"That's what you are here for. To entertain. You are entertainment. A payment for a debt." Her words are cold and cruel and I stumble back. I know Linda is tough, but I never thought she was cruel.

"Did my dad run up the debt in these rooms?" I ask the dreaded question.

"What does it matter?"

"It matters to me." My shouts have Linda closing the door behind her.

"Keep your voice down," she speaks through gritted teeth.

"Why? What else can you possibly do to me? Does Gerald know?"

Linda's lips tug up and she laughs. "Oh, I see. You think you mean something to Gerald?"

My face burns more at her mocking tone. Did I? Yes, I did.

"You are like Wendy and Candy to him. Money spinners." She steps closer and my heart cracks.

"You can leave now."

I move around Linda.

"I mean this place. The debt is cleared."

My hand is on the handle and I can't sort out everything I am feeling. *I'm free.* Tears fill my vision as I turn to Linda. "I can leave?"

"Your father's dead. So the debt died with him."

The smugness in Linda's voice dies slowly as she speaks. Saliva fills my mouth.

"You should just leave this place, Cara." Linda wavers and I can't speak. I'm out the door and moving into the club. The music, laughter and people all swirl around me as I move through the crowd. I get weird looks. People step out of my way as I stumble. My father is dead.

A hand grips my upper arm and I lash out, connecting with Linda's face. I blink and tears fall down my face. "Don't touch me."

The beat continues to pound, but it feels like everyone is watching us. Linda releases me and if she could breathe fire, I'm sure she would.

I don't think as I step into the hidden hallways and make my way back to my room. I don't remember walking here, but I'm standing in the bedroom in front of my bed. I want to do something. I want to cry, scream, something, but my body isn't reacting to any of it.

"Cara," I say my name out loud and something tightens in my stomach.

"Cara," I call louder and flinch at the harshness of my voice.

My hand strikes my face, the burn is instant. "Wake up," I tell myself as I strike my face again.

My legs lose their mobility and I find myself on the wooden floor holding onto the quilt. I don't know what is more horrifying, that I have no idea how I feel about my dad dying or that I don't want to leave this place. This place that twisted me up so tightly—until I broke. Broke in the worst way possible, I have feelings for my captor.

I'm disgusting.

Something sticky on my hair touches my chest. The man's cum. Laughter bubbles up my chest and I let it out. My hands tighten on the quilt that I rip from the bed. Something inside me sparks to life and I pull off all the bedding before opening my drawers and throwing my clothes everywhere. I pull the room apart until I'm breathless. Stepping into my wardrobe, I take every piece of material off the hangers. I pull a nightgown around me as I put my feet into a pair of sneakers. Taking one final look around the room, I slip through the secret door and make my way back to the club. I get a lot of stares as I walk through the front and out into the changing room. Something is going right. Candy's here. When she sees me in the mirror, she spins around.

"Holy Shit Cara. What happened?"

My throat burns again. "Could you give me a ride home?" I don't blink. I try to stuff all my emotions down.

"Of course, sweetie. I'm finished now in ten minutes." She stands up and walks to me. "Did something happen?"

"My dad died," I say.

Candy's hand covers her mouth. "I'm so sorry."

I look away from her watery eyes.

"We can go now." She takes my hand in hers. "Just give me a minute."

I nod as Candy disappears. I'm aware of all the new girls glancing at me. It feels surreal to be standing here feeling so out of place.

"You ready?" Candy's changed and is holding a handbag. I follow her out into a parking lot. We stop at a brown car and Candy unlocks my door first before she goes around to the driver's side. I get in and hate how my hands tremble as I put on the seatbelt. How long had I been here? I think it was weeks. Maybe months. It is like a time warp. I can't stop looking as we leave the castle behind in the rear-view mirror. Not just the castle, but Gerald.

"You want to give me directions," Candy questions, and it pulls me out of my head.

"Number seven. Dunaghmore Park," I rhyme off and my stomach twists painfully. Candy doesn't ask any more questions as she drives me home. When she pulls up outside the house, I don't want to get out.

"You want me to come in with you?" Candy asks.

I shake my head and turn to her. "No. it's fine. Thanks so much for giving me a lift."

She pulls me into a hug and I don't close my eyes. I don't allow myself to feel this comfort. "I'll be in touch." I unbuckle my belt and get out of the car. I don't look back as I open our small front black gate. The green grass on either side of the pathway is devoid of flowers or shrubs. A boot statue is the only thing at the front door. I lift it and pick up the spare key. Pushing it into the keyhole, I open the door and step into the darkened hall. Turning, I wave at Candy who's still sitting there. I flick on the lights and close the front door behind me. It takes a few seconds before I hear Candy's car leave.

I'm looking down the empty hall. My heart is pounding too hard. I need water. I walk into the kitchen, my leg connects with the table. I step away and flick on the light. The table has been moved away from the back door. He must have moved it after I left. *After he sold me.* A roar is building up inside me. I go to the press and take down a glass before filling it up. Sipping it slowly, I stare around the kitchen. It feels so small. So foreign to me. Placing the glass on the counter, I turn off all the lights and lock the front door before going upstairs. Some part of me wants to feel something about my father's death, so I go to his bedroom. His bed is made. All his clothes put away. His room doesn't produce any emotion about him. The only pain I'm feeling is my loss. I had no idea what to do now. A large part of me wants to go back to my room. My room in the castle.

There is something seriously wrong with me. I turn off the light in my dad's room and enter the bathroom. Running the bath, I strip off my clothes. The closet room in the castle was three times bigger than my bathroom. I feel like I can barely breathe here. Once the bath is full, I step into it. The water's piping hot and immediately turns my white skin pink. The constant pinch along my skin is what I focus on as I wash my body. Blue eyes so intense flash behind my closed eyelids, so I open them. But some twisted part of me seeks the darkness. I get out of the bath and turn off the lights before stepping back in and I smile. Everything here—in this moment—is possible. All the most intense emotions rise to the surface. Fear of what Gerald will do, excitement of what Gerald will do. *Gerald.* Tears make a path down my face as I finally admit to myself that I have feelings for him, whatever that makes me. I'm not sure, but I can't remove the fact of Linda telling me Gerald knew I was in the backrooms—and how it hurts me more than my father's death. Being let go hurt me even worse. I let a sob out and it finally allows me to grieve in the darkness where no one can judge me.

CHAPTER TWENTY

HIM

I'm in the library, seated behind my desk. My mind won't stop picturing Cara bent over it.

"It's just, we had a report that he was seen here."

I look at the Gardaí who sits in the chair across from me. "Yes, he was here. He was helping out around the castle. He wasn't the easiest to take directions so he quit."

The Gardaí scribbles the lies in his notepad. "When was this?" He asks looking at me over his notepad.

"We have so many staff coming and going. Let me think." I exhale loudly and sit back in my chair.

"It's really important that you try to remember the exact date."

I force a smile. "Of course, Gardaí. Tuesday last week." That was the last day he was on the property. Sticking even partially to the truth made this easier. "I don't like to speak out of turn, but it wouldn't do any harm to keep an eye on the father," I say.

The Gardaí sits forward. "You think he has something to do with his son's disappearance?"

I shrug and hold up my hands. "Yeah. It's silly. Forget I spoke."

"No, anything you can tell us would really help."

I nod. "His father was very abusive towards him. With his fists."

The Gardaí scribbles in his notepad. "Mickey told you that?"

It would be a hell of a lot easier to say yes. But me and Mickey would have had to be close for him to share that with me.

"No, his father was here with him, when we were ironing out the details about his job. He hit him in front of me for speaking out of turn. Mickey was afraid of him. I thought I might be able to help the boy." I look away from the Gardaí. "Poor kid."

The Gardaí closes his notepad. "Thank you, Mr. Norris. You have been more than helpful." I take the Gardaí's outstretched hand and shake it.

"Anything I can do to help."

He shakes the notepad at me before slipping it into his jacket pocket. "You've given us loads."

I walk the Gardaí out to the front of the property. Lights along the driveway light up his path as he climbs back into his car and leaves. I don't go back in until his tail lights disappear beyond the hill.

I make my way to the club. Linda is back to herself and I know she brought Cara to the club tonight. I told her to give Cara center stage. She's ready to shine. I need her presence right now. I don't want to think about Mickey rotting away in the forest. I feel like I've given the Gardaí enough to investigate Mickey's dad, and if they looked deep enough, they would find all his other ventures. It might be enough to overlook small details, like not finding his body.

The club is busy and I keep to the back, to the shadows. I still don't want Cara to see me. I'm not even sure why. If it's fear, or perhaps the power I feel at keeping that from her. B, who's been with us for a while, is on center stage. She isn't great and I scan the room for Cara or Linda. I see neither. I move along the back wall towards the bar. Simon and two other part-time staff members move quickly serving drinks. Each dancer that passes me smiles but I don't return them. I can't see Candy either. She is close to Cara. I wait until B steps off the center stage and the lights dim. I move around the room and cut her off at the changing rooms.

"Hi," she's panting as she looks up at me. There is always that slight look of fear in the dancer's eyes whenever I approach them.

"Have you seen Cara?"

Her brows pull together. "Cara? Yeah."

I stare at her.

"She's out back. In the boom boom rooms."

My stomach hollows out and I manage a nod to B, before I walk across the room. I don't bother with the shadows or trying to disguise myself. I need to get to Cara and get her out of there. The idea of anyone touching her has me moving faster. Damien takes one look at me and steps aside. I open each door and ignore the angry shouts and screams that sound from each room. Each door I open brings more panic. Where is she? I get to the final room and it's empty.

Maybe B was wrong. I go back to Damien, who doesn't turn as I close the door behind me.

"Where is Linda?" I ask him, looking out on the club. I still can't see her or Cara.

"In her office," Damien answers without moving his head.

I find Linda in her office, she doesn't seem surprised when I step in. I try to keep the rage that whirls inside me under control. But each passing second is making it harder.

"You sent Cara into the back rooms?"

Linda's holding a yellow file and closes it. "Yes." She places it on her desk and sits down. "This is my job. These girls are my…"

"Not Cara." My fist hits her desk and she jumps, startled. "What did she have to do?" I ask, not wanting to know, but needing to know.

"I'm not breaking my client's confidentiality."

"This is the final time Linda. What did she have to do?"

"Masturbation, that was it. I picked a simple one."

"No, you picked a degrading one."

Linda laughs and it's loud. "You kept her in a room like a dog. You have no right to come at me."

I push my hands into my pockets. Right now the only place I want them is around Linda's neck. If I started to squeeze, I wouldn't stop until she stopped breathing.

"It was more than that. Where is she now?"

Linda stares at me. Her eyes harden. "Are you telling me you have feelings for her?"

What I feel for Cara confuses to me. I'm not about to try to explain it to Linda. "Where is she?" My voice rises, and I'm unsure how much longer I can wait.

"Gone." Linda stands up now. "She was here to pay a debt. That debt died when her father died."

I feel like someone has taken all the air out of the room. "Gone. Gone where?"

"Gerald. You were becoming obsessed with this girl. Look at you. I don't recognise you anymore."

I turn away from Linda.

"It's better this way."

"For who?" Anger like I have never felt before floods my veins. "For you?" I take a step towards her. "For me?" She backs away. "But not for Cara. I want to kill you right now." I admit as Linda's back hits the wall.

"She's fine, Gerald. She's gone home to bury her father."

I stop advancing on her. "You told her that her father died?"

"Yes." Guilt coats Linda's face.

"How?" I ask and she can't look at me.

"How Linda?"

"I was angry," she shouts back.

I'm at her desk now, and I round it. "How?"

"When she was finished with Carl."

Linda screams as my fist smashes into the wall beside her face. Pain burns my hand and races up my arm.

"You're a vindictive, twisted bitch. Get out of my club."

Linda's fear scatters for a moment. "You're firing me?"

I step away before I hit her. "Get out."

She's shaking her head. "I'm in love with you, Gerald. I'm just jealous."

"You think I'd touch someone like you?"

She stands straighter now. "What is so special about her?" Her nose flares with jealousy.

"When I get back here you better be gone." I leave her office as she screams after me.

Cara's room is carnage. Sitting on her bed, I look around at the destruction and try to picture what she was feeling. The mess surprises me. I didn't think she would have come back here. There was nothing for her. Her anger was a visible thing. She must have been devastated at her father's death. She shouldn't have been. He had sold her. She was worth far more than that. My phone rings and I take it out immediately, wondering if it's her.

It's a silly error. She doesn't have my number. She doesn't know who I am. She ran the moment she had the chance. Can I really blame her?

"Jake, now is not a good time."

"You need to get out of there, now."

I stand up and step over all the scattered clothes. "Don't be worried, the Gardaí were already here. I pointed them in the direction of his father," I say as I leave the room. "You shouldn't be ringing me." I'm tired and my voice doesn't hold the anger it should at him ringing me.

"Listen to me, Gerald. This is not about Mickey."

I stop walking.

"Linda's gone off the deep end. She's reported you for keeping a girl captive in your house." There is a long pause. "Is it true?"

He won't judge me, I can say it to Jake. I really don't think he'll care. "No."

"Okay good. The Gardaí just passed the bridge, they're on their way."

"I know you said you didn't. But if there is someone in room twenty three I'd advise you to remove them."

My heart pounds as I rush back to Cara's room, shocked that Linda gave the room number. "There is no one to remove, but thanks for the heads up." I hang up and enter the room. I don't think, but just start putting all the clothes back in drawers and the wardrobe. I'm not great at making up the bed, but at least it doesn't look like the room was ransacked. I leave the room and remove my suit jacket to try to cool down my body.

"Marcus," I say into the phone when it rings. I hope I sound calm.

"Mr. Norris. There is a Gardaí Manning here to see you."

"You can escort him to the library. I'll be there shortly."

I hang up and enter my own room. Opening up the double doors to my wardrobe, I step in and turn on the lights. The third row down holds all my jackets. Taking a navy one off the hanger, I slip it on. Gardaí Manning is walking around the library. He isn't the same one who was here only a short time ago. He's looking at the books, just like Cara had.

"I'm very popular today," I say.

He turns around, opening his suit jacket. He steps down and reaches out a hand that I take. "I do apologize but we got a very serious complaint that we have to look into."

I point at the seat in front of my desk and he declines.

"This won't take long Mr. Norris. We had a complaint that you are holding a Cara Black here against her will."

"Can I ask who made such a complaint about me, Gardaí Manning?"

"I'm afraid not. But I would like to take a look around." Of course he would, and I'll allow him into Cara's room. I just won't make it easy.

"This establishment is private. You can search the area that's open to the public. I don't want to upset my clients. Do you understand Gardaí Manning?"

The Gardaí have been paid to turn a blind eye to the club. As long as everything is consensual, they always look the other way. It cost a lot, but having that free rein is what made this club the best in the country.

"I understand Mr. Norris, but someone being kept against their will is an entirely different thing. We were given a room number. If I'm allowed to see that room—and see it's empty—we can drop this matter."

I exhale loudly. "Fine. What is the room number?"

"Twenty three." He studies me closely as he says it, waiting to see if I flinch or panic.

"This way," I say calmly. I give him the scenic route. I'm a little impressed that Linda had the nerve to sell me out. Her anger is something I've experienced before, but that was a long time ago. A time when she didn't know me. She had been so broken down by her family and the system that it really didn't take much to bring her back up. Once I got her standing, I knew I had found something special in Linda. Someone who didn't really feel anymore. They had sucked the life out of her. Stripped her bare. But I gave her revenge, I gave her a job and her self-respect back.

Now stepping into Cara's room, my own anger returns at Linda's betrayal. "Room number twenty three. I don't have much time."

Gardaí Manning checks the wardrobe and the bathroom before taking a final look around the bedroom. He doesn't speak, just nods as he leaves the room. *Something is off.*

"The cameras in the room. What are they for?"

I grin at his hawk eye. "It's for the guests that request to watch themselves at a later date."

"Do you have the tapes from the last twenty-four hours?" We are now back at the library and I stuff my hands into my pockets.

"No. We only record when someone requests it."

"So the cameras are off now?"

I knew they were on. He knew they were on. "Yes. Now I really must get back to work."

He isn't happy, and something in his eye tells me he isn't letting this go. "Okay. Thank you for taking the time." He reaches out his hand and I take it. He doesn't let me go. "If I find out that any of this is true, I'll take it all down." He releases my hand and steps away. I watch him until he disappears around the bend of the hallway. I don't take kindly to threats. Especially from someone beneath my pay grade.

I return to Cara's room and remove all the cameras. No doubt when they find her she will spill everything that was done here. I need to get rid of all the footage that ties her to this place. I kept so much. Each visit she made. I have a file on her, close-ups of her face. Maybe Linda was right. I *had* become obsessed with her. With having her. Owning her. I didn't think when I touched her that she would become so alive, I didn't think it would jumpstart me either. She makes me feel things that I haven't felt in a long time.

Opening her wardrobe, I start to remove all the clothes. I need to remove her from this house. I just don't think I can remove her from my mind.

CHAPTER TWENTY-ONE

HER

The banging at the front door is persistent. I pull myself out of the bath and wrap my fluffy dressing gown around me. Whoever is at the door keeps knocking as I half run down the stairs. Turning on the lights, I open the door. It's a Gardaí. He removes his hat. It's something they do when they are delivering bad news. It must be about my dad.

"Come in." I open the door fully and he steps in. "You can go into the kitchen. I'll just be a moment."

"Take your time," he says with a nod before going into the kitchen. I race up the stairs and get into a pair of black pajamas. I don't bother brushing my hair, I want to get this part done and over with. I also realized that I hadn't even asked Linda how he died. Guilt swirls in my stomach as I skip down the stairs.

"Can I get you a tea or coffee?" I ask, folding my arms across my chest.

"No, this won't take long, Cara."

I don't sit down, but lean against the counter. The Gardaí is seated, but he moves his chair so he's facing me.

"We got a complaint that you were being held captive in Slane Castle."

I cough as the saliva catches in the back of my throat. *Someone reported it.* "Who made the complaint?" I ask, and the Gardaí tilts his head.

"That's an odd question to ask Cara, but that information is confidential. So, is it true?"

My eyes burn and my throat closes in on me. "No," I whisper.

"You seem upset." He's standing now.

"My father just died so…"

"Where have you been the last week?" he asks, and his tone snaps me out of my upset.

"What?"

"Your father died four days ago."

"And I can't be upset about it now?" I unfold my arms and look at his badge. "Gardaí Manning, I'm tired. I'd like you to leave."

"You can be upset, Cara. It's just…I called here each day and no one was at home. That's why, when I got the complaint about you being held captive, it made sense. What daughter wouldn't be here when her father died?"

"How did he die?" Tears trickle down my face.

Gardaí Manning puts his hat back on. "He drowned."

My heart stills as I can only imagine him fighting for air.

"He was drunk and fell into the Boyne."

I look away from Gardaí Manning.

"I'm sorry for your loss, Cara."

I swallow the grief that I'm feeling for the first time as the Gardaí lets himself out.

I always knew the drink would take him, I just never thought it would be due to falling into the Boyne River. I thought he would just go to bed drunk and his body wouldn't allow him to get back up.

I wipe the tears from my cheeks and straighten the chair that the Gardaí had been sitting on. Switching off the lights, I check the door again and go upstairs. My room looks like a little girl's room. I lie on my single bed and stare at the ceiling. The castle is like a dream. Gerald is like a dream, but also a nightmare. I can't decide which. Turning in the bed, I face the wall and crave my large double bed. I crave the smell. I'm back in the castle, but each creak pulls me awake. The house seems noisier than I remember.

My eyes snap open. This noise is different. My heart picks up and starts to race.

"Gerald?" I whisper, feeling silly.

"Yes."

I'm sitting up straight in the bed and I wish I had a lamp. His outline I can see. "What are you doing here?" My words sound breathless like I've been running. "How did you get into my house?"

Gerald brings the same emotions to the surface as he always does, fear mixed with excitement.

"I don't know why I'm here." His words are low.

My stomach drops. I'm not sure what I was expecting for him to say, that he missed me or he wanted to make sure I was okay after Carl.

"You sent me into those rooms." I can't stop the hurt that snakes its way around my words.

He hasn't moved and he doesn't respond. I tighten my hold on the quilt. "What do you want?" My heart pounds as I say the words.

He moves and I shuffle back until I hit the headboard.

"I just needed to see you."

His words secretly make me feel ten feet tall, but I don't allow him to see it. "Fine. You see me. Now leave."

He steps right up to my bed and sits on the edge. My heart pounds wildly.

"I didn't send you into those rooms, Cara. Linda did."

"But she said you agreed." I'm staring at him and I have no idea what I'm really feeling.

"She lied."

How could I possibly know that? He could be lying. Yet, he had never lied to me, or maybe he had.

His hand moves and rests on my leg. The quilt is dividing us, but the heat finds its way through the material and all the way to my skin where I feel it burn. With his other hand, Gerald drags the blanket down slowly and I release it from its death grip.

I hold my breath as he takes my face in his hands. I have a choice now, I can stop this. This is my home. I could scream, run, ring the Gardaí. When his lips touch mine all thoughts of leaving scatter as I grip his wide shoulders and pull him into me, deepening the kiss. I've never felt hungry for someone before, but this hunger with Gerald feels like it's consuming me. His hands slip under my pajama top. I don't have a bra on, his hand takes my breast easily, my nipples have hardened. I open the buttons and pull it off while breaking the kiss.

"Take off your clothes," I say, and he stands up and strips. When he returns, my hands roam warm flesh that shifts and flexes under my touch.

The single bed is awkward, but I get off and make him sit on the edge. Kicking out of my bottoms, I stand naked before him as I run my hands through his hair. In the safety of the darkness, I speak honestly.

"I want you." I move closer but Gerald stops me.

My heart bounces around my chest and I want to take my words back. I don't want this to stop.

"I want you too, Cara." He pulls me forward until I'm straddling him. His words fill me with a power that is transforming me. Reaching back, I direct his shaft into me and slowly move down until I take all of him. The sense of being stretched feels good. Gerald's hands burn my hips as he holds me and moves me up and down on his cock. I hold on to his wide shoulders as I move slowly, enjoying each stroke. My mind wanders to the dark part where I wonder when he gets sick of me and leaves. I'll be nothing, a shell. I move quicker, outrunning those thoughts. Bending my head, I touch my lips against Gerald's before flicking out my tongue and licking his lips. He grips my ass as he stands while still holding me in position, before turning and lying me on the bed. He thrusts hard and fast and I want to slow down. I want to savor this moment, but his frantic pace has me spreading my legs further for him, giving him as much access to me as possible. I'm pulling him closer, the want to have him has me digging my nails into him, trying to join us as he pounds into me. My tongue fills his mouth and I groan when his enters mine. His pace slows and I'm not ready to slow down. I'm pulling at his back, digging my nails in.

"More. I need more," I say through kisses.

His lips leave mine as he pulls out before slamming himself back into me. The motion gets quicker. The sound of flesh slapping against flesh has my nipples rock hard, Gerald bends his head and takes one in his mouth, but it slows his movements.

"No. Just fuck me," I say and he leans out and returns to his hard and heavy thrusts. I touch my own breasts and groan as the pain of squeezing my nipples has me wanting more pain.

"Harder," I demand. My headboard slams against the wall at each thrust and I don't hold back but moan and shout out my pleasure. Gerald's moans make mine louder and I'm riding so high that I don't want to come down. He pushes deeper, his hands pulling my hips closer to him. I squeeze my nipples harder and cry out.

"I'm going to come." Gerald's declaration has me focusing on him as he rushes to the finish line, and I spill my juices all over his cock that jerks and releases its seed inside me. This time, the moment I come down my body aches everywhere. But it's a good ache. He pulls out of me slowly but still remains between my legs.

"You're perfect."

I'm smiling at his words. I'm not sure he can see me in the darkness. I can make out his outline, but that's it.

"Can I see you?" I ask and he moves quickly. I sit up and pull the blanket around my naked body. My heart sinks as he starts to get dressed.

"What are you so afraid of?" He doesn't answer. I am starting to see a pattern with him. He leaves when something doesn't suit him.

"Okay, you're going to run now, but I can't keep doing this. I don't care what you look like. I like you." The confession has my stomach tightening.

It also has him pausing. He has his trousers back on and he is ready to zip them up. He resumes getting dressed. Pulling a black t-shirt over his head, he pulls on his shoes.

"If you leave here, don't ever come back." My throat and eyes burn. There is another pause and I'm praying for him to speak. He can say anything at this stage and I'll listen, but he doesn't and I want to tell him it's okay, come back. But some part of me that still has respect for myself keeps me quiet as he leaves my room. I listen through the blood pumping in my ears to the closing of the front door. I sob into my quilt and once again I'm left wondering what is wrong with me.

I don't sleep much and no matter how much coffee I drink, it doesn't wake me up. I got a phone call this morning from Des, our local funeral director. My father will be cremated today. They arranged it since I hadn't. He offered to change things, but I was happy to go ahead with it. Dressed in a black dress, I refill my coffee for the sixth time. The house is so quiet. Not that my dad was around much, but for the first time, I'm aware of the silence. I was getting used to the music of the club, the chatter with the girls. The silence of the house feels unnatural. I take the black shawl and my bag from the counter. I need to leave now or I'll miss my father's funeral. The ring of the front door has my heart pounding and I walk to it slowly.

The possibility that it could be Gerald has me tensing.

"Hi."

Disappointment courses through me, but I try to reel it in. "Hi." I want to ask Candy what she is doing here.

"I thought you might need a friend today." I notice she's dressed in black too, seeing her fully clothed is so different from her half-naked self.

"How did you know?" I step out onto the porch and pull the door closed behind me.

"Gerald told me."

The mention of his name has me snapping my attention to Candy. She grins at my reaction.

"Are you guys together?"

My face burns. "No. Not at all."

Her laughter tells me I'm not so convincing. It dies down as I stare out onto the front lawn. Who was going to cut it now? It was the one job he actually did.

"Do you want me to come with you? Or maybe you have someone else?" Candy glances behind me like someone else might step out of the house.

"I'd really love it if you came."

Candy drives to the funeral home, which is only five minutes away. I had intended to walk. Once we arrive, Des is there to greet us. It's sad that only three other people are here. Three faces that I know. Three alcoholics. At least they came. They each approach me and shake my hand. The last one, I can't remember his name, is drunk right now.

"I'm so sorry." His loud words comfort me. They take the sting out of this situation.

"I'm sorry for your loss, too. I think he spent more time with you than me," I answer honestly as my vision blurs. Candy's arm wraps around my shoulders as Des moves out onto the floor.

"Anything you want to say?" He asks me and I have nothing to say, so I shake my head and sit down with Candy. The local priest, whose name I can't remember because I don't go to church, starts the prayers.

My mind won't stay in the present. I hate that I can't think of anything happy or positive. My father never put his hands on me, but I was always minding him. Putting him to bed. Cleaning up after him. The bills were my responsibility. I never really had friends, I was always too embarrassed to bring them back to my home. It's clean, but mostly bare. So I learned to keep to myself, and I found friends between the pages of books.

Candy's hand fills mine and I realize I'm crying. I squeeze her hand back in thanks. Maybe that's why I clung to Gerald. He was my first of many things. I cry harder and when one of dad's drunken friends sits beside me to comfort me, I can't stop the laughter. If they knew I was crying for me and not him, they would think I'm a monster.

"Let it all out," Candy's encouragement has me sobering up.

"I'm okay," I tell both Candy and dad's friend who's now sitting beside me. The priest fell silent while I broke down and I look up at him now to let him know to continue. He gives me a look of pity before he continues. I most certainly look like a grieving daughter.

Curtains behind the priests move back and dad's coffin is there. We stand as it goes up in flames. I watch it until the curtains pull back into place.

"Let's go have a drink for our friend." Dad's friends all band together. I wonder if they even knew that he drowned because he was so drunk.

"Would you like to join us?" The one that had sat beside me asks. I give his arm a squeeze. The tweed material of his mustard jacket is harsh on my palm.

"I'm good. But have one for me."

He laughs. "That I can do."

They leave and Candy links her arm with mine but doesn't say anything about the empty funeral home or the three drunk men. I feel I owe her an explanation.

"My dad was an alcoholic," I say

"I know sweetie, and I'm sorry."

I glance at Candy, wondering how she could know that. "I saw him at the club and he had that look."

We leave the funeral home. "How did you know he was my dad?" I ask. As we step outside into the fresh air, a drink didn't sound so bad now.

"He stood out."

Now I stop and look at Candy. "What do you mean?"

She shrugs. "I don't know. He wasn't like our normal clientele. He just sat at the bar and drank himself silly."

"He never went out into the back rooms?"

"No."

I don't think Candy could possibly understand the relief I'm feeling. I pull her into a tight hug.

"Thank you for telling me," I say.

She smiles. "No problem. How about a coffee?"

"That sounds great."

We go into the local hotel for a coffee. There is only one other coffee shop and it's already full. The hotel is quiet enough as we sit down and order our drinks.

"How are you holding up?"

I thank the waitress as she lays out our coffees before answering Candy. "I'm okay, I think." I can't tell her how I really feel. She would think I am weird.

"Any word on Wendy?" I ask instead, and I can see relief in Candy's eyes at the change in topic. Death is an uncomfortable topic for most, so I am glad to change it. I am also very grateful that Candy is here for me.

"She's doing good. I heard she's in rehab and getting better. Me and B are going to visit her next week if you want to come."

"Yes. I'd love that. Not love it." I shake my head. "I just mean I'll go with you guys." I have friends for the first time. Friends who invite me to things. It might be a rehab, but I don't care.

"So there was a huge shakedown at the club." Candy smirks. "Linda got fired."

The blood drains from me. "Why?"

"Nobody really knows. But the biggest thing is that Linda isn't the owner. We were all told she was, but it's come out that Gerald owns everything. Which is crazy because he's always just been the security."

"Wow. He seems to like hiding his identity. I wonder why?"

"I'm not sure why. Maybe because it's a strip club and women are more trusting of women."

"Yeah, maybe." I don't believe that. I don't know what to believe, but the fact I never saw Gerald, and now he is hiding who he actually is, makes me even more suspicious than ever. We chat for a while longer. After two more coffees, I'm all coffeed out and am ready to go home. Lying down and just sleeping seems like a good idea since I didn't sleep much last night.

Candy drives me back.

"I can't thank you enough for today. I don't think I could have gotten through it so easily without you," I say as we pull into my estate.

"Do you want me to come in with you?" Candy offers and I reach across and squeeze her hand.

"No, but thanks. I think I'll get some sleep."

Candy stops the car and she's staring at my house. "Gerald's car."

I look out the window to see a brand new Audi parked in front of my house. "That's Gerald's car?" I ask as my stomach squeezes. "But it's daylight," I say.

Candy laughs. "Yeah, cause it's daytime."

I let out a shaky laugh. "Yeah. I'm just tired. I better go in."

"Okay. If you need me, just ring."

"Thanks, Candy." She had put her number into my phone at the hotel. I close the car door and stare up at my house. Gerald is in there somewhere and I am going to see his face.

CHAPTER TWENTY-TWO

HIM

TWELVE HOURS BEFORE

After leaving Cara's house, I pull up to the castle. Light shines from random windows. I don't want to go in. I want to go back to Cara, but her questions are too much right now. I consider going to the club, but that's just another mess. Parking the car I make my way to my private quarters. I know someone is here the minute I step in. I can smell perfume and alcohol. Only one person would be brazen enough to be in my home.

"I thought I told you to leave." I flick on the lights and she's sitting on my couch.

"You were with her," her slurred words sober up some of my rage.

"That's none of your business. You need to leave now, Linda." For old time's sake, I will keep my cool.

"But I am home." She stands up, the bottle of brandy nearly three quarters gone. "This is where I live."

I exhale loudly before walking to her. "Give me the bottle."

She holds it behind her back. "No."

She leans in and tries to kiss me. I easily sidestep and take the bottle. "You're a mess," I say as I walk to the sink and pour the contents of the bottle down it.

"You made me like this."

My anger shatters and I throw the bottle into the sink. "This." I turn to her. "I didn't make this weak, babbling woman."

Linda stands taller and tries to stop the tremble of her lip by biting it. "I love you, Gerald." She wipes tears from her cheeks. "I think I always have."

"You have no idea of what love is," I say.

"And you do?" Her anger returns.

"No. I think we are pretty damaged," I answer honestly.

She smiles and takes a few wobbly steps towards me. "Exactly." She sniffles. "So we get each other. We are made for each other." Her hands touch my shoulders and I gently remove them.

She sobs at my touch. "We are bad for each other. You can start a life anywhere, Linda. I'll give you whatever you want."

Her eyes flicker to me. "I want you."

Shaking my head, I release her hands. "I don't want you."

Her hand connects with my face and I allow it. "You did this to me," her roar is accompanied by another slap that I allow.

She tries to strike me again, but I grab her hand. "That's enough."

She pulls her hands out of mine. "I've been living here, so I've nowhere to go."

"You should have told me. You can't just move into my home."

She laughs as she stumbles back to the couch. "But I did. Gerald." She sings my name at the end. When she reaches the couch, she lies down.

"I'm sorry for ringing the Gardaí. That was in bad taste."

I grin. Bad taste. She could get me arrested.

"Just get some sleep." She would have to leave tomorrow. Her being here isn't good for either of us anymore.

"Don't leave me." Her words are low and mumbled as she starts to drift off to sleep. I pick up my suit jacket and put it on over my t-shirt.

Taking the blanket off the back of the couch, I cover her with it and leave. The club is alive and full. For the first time in a long time, I don't lurk along with the shadows but step out into the middle of the floor. Once, everyone looked at me with fear, now they see me differently since they all found out I own the place. I hate it. I've never created this for money. I did it to destroy this place—to taint it—but it's popular, and it just kind of grew into this all by itself. Linda proved to be a fantastic leader, so one night she said it was hers and I allowed it to stick. I didn't mind taking a back seat in all this. After a while, the money was the driving force, but it started off with bad intentions.

"I'm glad to see you didn't get arrested." Jake slaps me on the shoulder. He's the only person who's looking at me the way he always has. "I need a drink."

I have no idea why he's here. He's brought me so much trouble, but right now a drink doesn't sound bad. Simon places a bottle of brandy on the counter, along with a glass. "One more glass," I say to Simon as Jake drags a stool beside me.

"Seen Linda earlier."

I pour out our two drinks. "Yeah?" I say sliding him a glass. I look at him now.

"She's in a really bad place, man." He sounds concerned.

"Maybe she could stay with you for a while," I suggest.

"Nah, she hates my guts."

I click my glass against his. "That makes two of us."

He laughs. "She's in love with you, man."

I drink down my brandy and refill my glass.

"Rough night?" Jake's looking at me now like he's only just now seeing me.

"Yeah, something like that."

"How's Cara?" Simon's been wiping the same spot since I sat down. I'm aware that he's been watching me, waiting for an opening to speak.

"Great," I answer, not liking his interest in Cara.

"Who's Cara?" Jake grins.

"A dancer," I say while still looking at Simon, who hasn't returned to his work. "I don't pay you to stand around." He takes his cloth down to the other end of the counter.

Jake sniggers. "You put him in his place."

Irritation circles under my skin. "I can't seem to put you in yours, Jake."

His smile dissolves. "I'm not a staff member, Gerald." His words are biting.

"If you were, I'd fire you." I finish off my brandy. I didn't come here to chat. I wanted a drink. "I've got to go," I tell Jake and he grabs the bottle of brandy and pours himself a glass.

I return to the castle and get a fresh bottle of brandy. I drink it as I walk through the hallways. A party is alive on the top floor, but I've no interest.

Taking the elevator, I make my way to the gallery. The doors open with a ding and I step out and take a long swallow of brandy. The painting of my grandfather mocks me. He won. He always said I was a fuck up. He's right. Everything around me is falling apart. The only way I could get someone to like me was to lock them in a room. I take another large swallow before I peg the bottle at the painting.

"It was me. Anything that you couldn't find. I'd taken." I grin up at the painting. "Your glasses, your favorite cane, I broke that and threw it in the river. I took your money. I took your home." My voice rises as I advance on him. "I took your life, old man." His face smiles down at me.

"You think you won?" I laugh and reach for the picture. It wobbles on the wall. "We'll see who's laughing now." The frame cracks as it hits the marble floor. A light flickers on the wall where the painting once hung. I drag my grandfather's sorry ass outside, checking my pockets I take out the lighter. His lighter, his initials. "Smile at this," I say before dropping it. The painting instantly goes up in flames, and I laugh as I watch his face melt. "Oh yeah!"

I'm aware of the alarm going off, and the blue lights that are flashing in the distance. They are getting closer to me as the Gardaí cars come over the hill. I laugh as they approach.

"No need to worry. Nothing has been robbed."

My hands are pulled behind my back. "What are you doing?"

"You're under arrest."

I yank my arms and smile when I come face to face with Gardaí Manning.

"I'm starting to think you have a thing for me." I grin.

"Put out the fire," he calls to one of his officers.

"That's my fucking painting. You will let it burn. Touch it and you die."

The officer pauses and I grin at Manning, who walks away from me and takes the fire extinguisher from the officer. He extinguishes the fire.

"Put him in the car."

"This is my property," I remind them all.

"Drunk and disorderly. That's what I can—☐and will—charge you with."

I'm placed in the back of the Gardaí car and taken away from the house. But I feel good.

The cell I am placed in is empty and I lie down on the hard bench. "Is there anyone you want to ring?" Gardaí Manning asks through the bars.

I think of Cara. "No. I'm good here."

"Suit yourself."

He leaves me alone and all I want to do is sleep. And surprisingly, I do for the first time in a long time. I sleep like a baby. When I wake up, my body aches from the hard bench.

Manning is standing at the bars drinking a cup of coffee. "Don't you ever go home?" I ask him as I widen my eyes and stretch.

"You want to make a phone call now?"

"Yeah, I do." I'm ready to go home now. The sleep did me good.

"When I've finished my coffee." Manning takes his sweet time. An hour passes and he's at his desk, the mug has to be empty at this stage. Cara's father is being cremated this morning, I informed Candy to be with her, but I also wanted to be there. Now it looks like that won't happen.

"Any chance of making that phone call?" I ask as nicely as I can.

"Are you still here?" He stands up from his desk and smirks. He slips the key into the lock and lets me out.

"You can use the phone on my desk."

So he can trace the call. There is really only one person I can ring.

"Gerald," Linda sounds really rough.

"I'm at Slane Gardaí Station, I need you to bail me out."

"Yeah, of course. I'll be there soon."

Manning is staring at me and I don't look away from him. Placing the receiver of the phone down, I sit in the chair that's in front of his desk.

"Who was that you called?" He is testing me.

"Linda, a very close friend."

"Girlfriend?"

"Just a friend."

He doesn't ask any further questions and Linda arrives. She looks like shit. The large black sunglasses that she slips onto her face don't hide the after effects of last night. My own eyes hurt as I step out into the light.

We don't speak as we walk to her car. She starts the engine and pulls out from the curb. I know she's going to start and my head can't take it.

"Let's forget about last night," I say.

"Yeah. I'd like that."

I stare out the window thinking of Cara. She's at her dad's funeral now. I hope she's okay.

"You still need to leave," I say to the window.

"Yeah, I know. And I will."

I glance at Linda. I can't see her face, but I'm grateful she isn't making this hard.

"I had the mess taken care of this morning." She speaks but still doesn't look at me.

"Thank you."

We pull into the long driveway that leads up to the castle. "You can stay with Jake for a while until you get sorted."

Linda glances at me. "Not happening."

I grin. I don't blame her. "Whatever money you need just let me know."

We pull up to the castle and Linda doesn't go any further. "I'm not going in, but this is goodbye for now."

My stomach tightens. She is all I have known for so long. Everything has changed so much. I know it is time we moved on, but letting go isn't easy. "You'll stay in touch?" I ask her and she lifts off her glasses.

"Yeah. I'm sorry for everything." She reaches across and hugs me. I hug her back. "I'm going to miss you." She admits. "Now get out."

I grin at her, but I can see her pain as I get out of her car and close the door. She puts the glasses back on and drives off.

Once I shower, I make the decision that I need to see Cara and try this relationship thing. I'm nervous, which isn't something that happens to me often. The last time I was this nervous was when the coroner was determining my grandfather's cause of death. I remember waiting for the news, waiting for sirens, but instead, they said it was just natural causes.

I stare at myself in the mirror. The black shirt and slacks make me look like I'm going to a funeral. Taking out a dark blue jumper, I place it over the shirt before getting my car keys and phone. I am going to go to her house and finally let her see me.

CHAPTER TWENTY-THREE

HER

The key doesn't go into the lock on the first try. I need to control the tremble in my hand. I told him last night it didn't matter what he looked like, so I need to try to relax. I exhale and get it right this time. Pushing open the door, I step into the hall and enter the kitchen. I'm smiling as my heart kicks up a beat. The fact he is willing to show me his face is what is making me so nervous. He wants me to see him. No one is in the kitchen. I check the sitting room, but it's empty too. I'm giddy with each step I take.

"Gerald?" I call as my stomach trembles.

"Yes."

I pause on the stairs as he answers me. Jesus, he is really here. I continue climbing the stairs.

"You know it's bright outside?" I'm trying to calm my pounding heart as I reach the landing.

"I know."

My bedroom door is half closed.

"I'm nervous," I say, staring at the wooden door.

"Me too."

His answer has me biting my lip. "I buried my dad today," I say while placing my hand on the door.

"I'm sorry, Cara. I wanted to be there for you."

I nod to the wooden door. "I felt like some kind of monster. I cried, but not for him. I cried for me."

"That doesn't make you a monster. It makes him one."

My head snaps up at his answer. "You do know that you shouldn't speak ill of the dead."

"You're stalling, Cara."

I give a nervous laugh. *I am.* This is so much easier—just talking through the door.

"Okay."

I push the door open and step into my bedroom that once was small but now is tiny. Gerald takes up too much of my room. My heart stills before it gallops and I'm smiling at him. Sweat dampens my hands.

"Hi." I'm taking him all in, but trying to do it slowly. He's gorgeous, and he's making me nervous with how he's staring at me.

He gets up off my bed and I step back, hitting the wall. He's too much. Blue eyes consume me.

"Hi." His tone is low.

I swallow. He's perfect. "Why? Why couldn't I see you before?"

His thick dark hair has a slight wave in it, it's the first time I've noticed it.

"It was easier for me to come to you and not have you see me." He takes another step closer to me.

I reach up and touch his face. "I would have been more obedient if I'd seen your face," I say.

His laughter has my stomach erupting with butterflies. It's a beautiful sound. His hand touches my face and I close my eyes and lean into the warmth of his flesh. He allows me to soak up his warmth, his smell. Turning my head into his hand, I plant a kiss on his open palm, before opening my eyes and looking at him from under my lashes. My heart jumps.

"You're beautiful, Gerald," I say.

A muscle twitches in his jaw. "There is so much about me you don't know." His eyes search my face. I think he's waiting for me to run.

"I know. There's a lot about me you don't know."

He grins and a smile spreads across my face.

"That's why I'm here. I want us to get to know each other. But, it's not going to be easy, Cara."

His eyes have darkened and I already know that Gerald will be complicated. But I kind of like that about him.

"You won't like everything you hear about me. There are some things that I can't change." His brows pull down as he speaks and his eyes darken further.

I place another kiss on his palm and his attention returns to me. I smile at him and his eyes lighten. "That's okay, Gerald. We can navigate our way through this."

I want to kiss him so badly, I want to have him inside me. I want all of him. The good, the bad, the dark, and the light. It doesn't matter to me. I want this man.

His other hand slides into my hair as he tilts my head, his eyes dart to my lips. "There's no going back now, Cara. Are you sure about this?"

His promise terrifies me, it sounds so definite. "Yes," I answer while standing up on the tip of my toes and pressing my lips against his. My hands find their way into his thick hair as I push my tongue into his warm mouth. I groan into his mouth. His fingers graze the side of my breasts and it's an instant reaction, my body tightens and a shiver assaults me.

Gerald's fingers touch the zipper and he drags it down slowly, his thumb dragging along after the zipper sending electricity through me. Wetness pools between my legs and I push my body harder against his. I can feel his excitement through his trousers.

As he turns me, I bump into the wall. The room is so much smaller than what we are used to. "I wish we were at the castle," I say between kisses.

I squeal as Gerald picks me up and places me on the floor, he hasn't removed his hand from my waist. I'm looking up into dark blue eyes, my core tightens.

"Why's that?" He asks, he's panting while his eyes search my face. His hands reach down and take the hem of my dress that he pulls up over my head.

"More space," I answer while reaching for his buttons.

"I can work in tight spaces."

I bite my lip at his words while I open his trousers and push them down his hips; he wriggles out of them and kicks them off. His stomach is toned with well-defined muscles. I want to touch them.

I give in and run my hand across his stomach before moving up to his head. He holds himself up above me as I touch every bit of flesh and muscle. He's perfection. My hands trail up to his face. He's mine. My stomach tightens again as I stare at him. My pulse quickens and heat enters my face.

"Kiss me," I command. He does, his tongue demanding entry into my mouth, I allow it. He lowers his body until it's pressed against mine, his erection prodding against my stomach. I spread my legs further, just wanting him inside me.

Gerald's lips leave mine as he kisses my jawline and continues to plant kisses down my neck. I suck in my stomach as he presses a kiss beside my belly button. His strong hands pull down my underwear before he pushes my legs far apart.

"I want you inside me," I tell him.

His wicked grin has my heart kicking up. I moan as he dips his head and pushes his tongue into my pussy. My hands find his hair and I hold his head between my legs, wanting him deeper. He does, and I groan. His tongue is replaced with his fingers as he licks my clitoris. I push my body up, not able to stay still. Gerald removes his fingers from inside me and crawls back up my body. His erection feels even larger as it pushes against my stomach once again. He holds his fingers to my lips. I can see the sheen off them. I flick out my tongue and lick while staring at him. His tongue runs along his fingers and I twitch as our tongue's meet while we suck my juices off his fingers. My lips slam against his, I can't take much more. His wet face turns me on and I grip his shoulders, trying to pull him closer. His mouth leaves mine once again as he kisses my neck before moving to my breasts. Rolling my nipple between his fingers, he works the other one with his tongue. My dampness has spread to the inner part of my thighs.

"Please, Gerald," I beg.

His teeth nip my nipple and I inhale quickly. He raises his head while placing his cock at my entrance.

"You want this?" He asks.

I'm nodding like a madwoman. "Yes, please."

His wicked grin is back as he pushes the tip in and I groan. "I love that sound." His words are accompanied with another push inside me.

He's filling me and I take every inch of him inside me. Reaching up, I brush my palm against his hard nipples. He pushes deeper and I squeeze them. The more I squeeze, the harder he fucks me. I'm glad we are on the ground as he pounds his cock into me. He doesn't hold back and I love the savagery of his movements. The ache of my stretched legs and the burn of the carpet on my back arouses me further. I pull his nipples harder and he rears his head back and groans; I tighten myself around him and his release fills me. I get my own release only seconds later and he continues to move slowly inside me as my body jerks. He's moving long after we have both come.

"I think you can stop now." I smile up at him. Heat taints my cheeks.

His movements cease and he removes himself. It's always awkward after sex. He normally leaves me, so when he gets up I'm expecting it. Maybe our thing will be sex. I'd rather have Gerald in any form than not have him at all.

My eyes widen as he picks me up and carries me to my bed. I don't know what to say as he climbs into my single bed. We both have to turn sideways to fit. He doesn't spoon me, he keeps me facing him as he drags the quilt over us. My chest burns and I swallow, not wanting to start crying. One strong arm wraps around me.

"What are you thinking?"

I glance up at him, into his handsome face, and I can't help but touch it. "How nice this is," I say.

His smile has me smiling.

"This is a first for me," he confesses.

"I knew you were a virgin."

He laughs and when he stops he smiles before speaking. "Holding someone."

I want to sit up, but if I move, I will fall from the bed. "You've never held someone after sex?" I really find that hard to believe, but then again, with Gerald, I don't. "Have you ever had a relationship?"

"No. There are a lot of firsts for me."

My heart swells and I can't stop the tug of my lips. "Me too."

He grows quiet and I watch his eyelids flutter closed. Long black eyelashes rest against his cheeks. He's all angles and muscles. My core twitches and I want to silence it and just enjoy being here in his arms.

"Why are you staring?"

I flinch as his eyes open. "Am I not allowed?"

"You can look at me whenever you want." His lips find mine and he plants a soft kiss on them. It's feather light, but it has the power to reach deep down and stir something new inside me. Fear at him leaving me starts to drip like a broken tap.

"Do I still work at the club?" I jump in feet first.

"Not as a dancer." He tightens his hold on me. "I don't want anyone else near you."

I smile at his possessive tone. "What about the back rooms?"

His jaw tightens. "You want to work there?" He sounds horrified.

"No. I'm asking if you'll close them down."

His face softens and he touches my lips with his thumb. "No."

"But they're wrong, Gerald," I say. I don't want to start off with all the negatives, but it's something that bothers me. I can live with the dancing, but the boom boom rooms don't sit right with me.

"Was it wrong when I made your fantasy come true?"

My chest burns. A part of me can't believe he would bring that up. But I try to act like a grownup and consider his question. "No. Because I wanted that."

He nods. "My clients want their fantasies to come true. Every person in every room has given their consent. No one is ever forced. What Linda did to you was wrong, Cara. If I could change it, I would."

My eyes burn, but I swallow down the emotion.

"I need you to understand that the club, the back rooms, they are a part of me."

I nod. "I know." Maybe they were a part of me too now. They say there is light and darkness in us all and we go through life believing it. But I don't think everyone truly ever sees their own darkness, I found mine at the hands of Gerald and for that I'm grateful.

I touch his face now. Just like him, my darkness makes my light burn brighter. My lips touch his.

"I was thinking...maybe you can give me a private tour of the castle?"

His perfect smile returns. "Look at you, calling in favors already."

I laugh.

"Tomorrow I will take you on our first date."

Our first date.

"My first date ever," I say, but my body is buzzing with excitement. Tomorrow feels like forever away. "Do we have to wait until tomorrow?"

"No. We can go now if you want."

Just like that, we can make a decision. It's weird not having to consider anyone else. Not even my father.

"I'll wait." I tighten my hold on Gerald as I let my mind wander to my father. He doesn't ask me why I've gone quiet. He just holds me like he understands what's wrong.

The heat and protection from Gerald's hold silences my busy mind, and I drift into a soft sleep.

CHAPTER TWENTY-FOUR

HIM

*T*he rain is coming down heavily. It makes driving difficult. Like, when you're driving in snow and it feels like you're speeding through the galaxy. The rain is just like that. I pull over, waiting for the worst to pass.

In the rearview mirror, I see a man huddled against the rain. He has pulled a hoodless jacket over his head. The wind seems strong as he keeps favoring his left side. The river rages along the bank and the low railing won't stop his fall. I'm not someone who interferes, but I don't want to witness someone's death. I don't have a jacket, and I hesitate at the door. I could just stop watching and let nature take its course. I get out of the car hoping Karma is watching my good deed.

"Do you need a lift?" I call. The rain is painful as it pelts down on top of me. The man continues to stagger. The wind has nothing to do with him favoring his left side. He's drunk.

"Christ." I slam the car door and pull my suit jacket over my head. "I'll give you a lift," I say the moment I get close enough.

He peeks at me through his jacket. "You." He lets his jacket go and the rain pounds down, soaking him in seconds. "Where is my daughter?" Through his drunken state I can hear his loss. But he doesn't deserve her.

"She's happy," I tell him. "Do you want a lift or not?" I'm not going to stand here, I'm already soaked enough.

"I want her back." His arm grips mine and I shook him off.

"No."

"I'll find a way to clear my debt." He's reaching for me again, trying to clutch on to me.

"You're a drunk. You will never be able to clear it." I push him back and let my jacket down. There is no point in trying to keep the rain off.

"Take me instead."

I laugh. "Go home, old man."

He isn't going to take a lift and I'm done standing in the rain.

"I remember you as a boy."

I keep walking.

"He couldn't beat the darkness out of you."

I pause and clench my fists.

"You let my daughter go." He's wobbling dangerously close to the railing. One wrong step and he'll find himself rolling down the bank and into the raging water.

There's no traffic around, and the rain has created a curtain around us. I walk back to Cara's father.

"Okay," I say.

He looks at me through his drunken eyes that have gone wide. "Really?"

I reach out my hand to his. "You have my word."

"Thank you." He places his hand in mine.

"My grandfather was an evil man."

Cara's dad's eyes widen further and he tries to pull his hand from mine, but I don't let go. I take a step towards him, forcing him back as I spoke. "He beat the darkness into me old man." I take another step and squeeze his hand. "She's mine," I say, before pushing him and releasing his hand. He's off-kilter as I walk back to my car. I can hear his scream as he falls over the railing. I hear the splash as his body hits the water. I get into my car, soaking my seat with my wet clothes. I'm close to the castle. Turning the car on, the engine purrs to life. I flick on the lights and they cut through the rain that seems to have eased off. Pulling away from the curb, I continue my journey home.

"This is the piano room." I walk around the large room that solely holds the black piano. I can play it, but I never do.

I love watching Cara as I take her into each room. She twirls, her mouth half open, her eyes alive. "It's amazing; I've never been to this part of the castle." Her eyes settle on me.

"It isn't open to the public." It is a room I actually like. "My mother taught me how to play."

Cara walks over to the piano and runs her fingers along each key. "Can you play me a song?" She glances at me from under her lashes.

"I will one day. Just not right now."

She looks like an angel today in her white summer dress. She holds still as I walk up to her and take her face in my hands and kiss her softly on the lips. I take my time with the kiss, exploring her lips. I'm trying to be more patient with her and with myself.

"That was nice." She's smiling, but still has her eyes closed. I haven't released her face as she opens her eyes and her smile widens. "I could get used to those type of kisses."

"Good. I plan on giving you lots more of them." I kiss her nose before taking her hand and continuing our tour of the house. Each room holds memories, each one worse than the next. Each room Cara steps into, I watch her take it all in, and I love how she sees it. It's how it should be seen. It's just tainted for me.

"The coin room?" She raises a brow. "Like, seriously?"

I smile. "Yes. This was my grandfather's favorite room." It was forbidden. His jewel. The one thing I never touched. As I walk through it now, with Cara at my side, I can see the beauty of the room.

"Every side of a coin has another side," I say the words I had heard a million times before. "My grandfather used to say people were like coins. Once you flip it in the air, you have no idea how it will fall. It's the journey the coin takes that will determine which way it falls." I run my hand over all the glass cabinets that are filled with so many different coins. "Good or bad, madness or genius. Yeah, he loved to toss a coin for lots of different reasons."

Cara's hand fills mine and her eyes shine with sorrow, like she knows the pain of this room. "I don't need a coin to know you're a good man."

I want to believe her. So I choose to. Leaving the room behind, I take Cara out to the gardens where I continue the tour. It's a happier place.

A place where I might be a better person.

A happier person.

All because of Cara.

My Cara.

THE END

I hope you enjoyed *Dark*.

Darker is the next book in the Boyne Club Series.

Read Damien and Maria's story.

You can download HERE: https://author-vicarter.com/products/dark

Or scan the code below:

Or read on for a sneak peek:

DARKER

CHAPTER ONE

The cold steel burns under my palm as I push the double doors open. The click of my heels join the beat of my heart. I'm pushing the boundaries with Damien, but I refuse to be ignored.

"Mrs. Callan."

I suppress a smile as Terry scrambles around the lone counter, trying to stop me with a raised hand.

"Please, Mrs. Callan, just let me tell him you're coming." I glance over my shoulder as he scours the desk in his panic for the phone.

"He's in a meeting." His final attempt to slow me down doesn't work. Nothing can stop me. I won't be ignored.

The area grows smaller—and my heart beats faster—as I push down on the gold handles and enter his office. He's in mid-sentence, talking to three other men who all turn, their eyes take in every inch of me. I hold my pose and let them.

The phone on Damien's desk rings with persistence.

"I'm in a meeting," Damien grinds out the words as he leans back in his chair.

"I need to go shopping." I haven't released the door handle and it's keeping me grounded under his gaze. He's always been easy on the eyes, but as he grew, I found myself appreciating him more and more.

Damien sits forward in his chair. I glance at his other colleagues who haven't taken their eyes off me. Capturing the attention of men I have mastered, from years of understanding that our bodies are the forbidden fruit they seek. They'll never have me, but that doesn't stop me from leading them to believe they could.

The one man I could never entice with my curves, and revealing ways, and too much skin, sits in front of me now with a warning flashing in his green eyes. I read the warning loud and clear, and I have a moment of uncertainty. I raise a brow.

"That's what I pay Andrew for." He doesn't release me from his stare as he cuts off the persistent ring of the phone.

"I know. I'm looking at her." He places the phone back in the receiver.

"Andrew is out sick." I pull in my bottom lip and can see the men shift. So easy.

Damien works a muscle in his jaw and I don't move. I won't be dismissed.

"Shall I go myself?" I sing sweetly and turn on my high black heels. The short leather skirt doesn't leave much to the imagination.

Terry frowns at me as I step into the lobby. The three men from the meeting pass me slowly, each one taking a peek. Curiosity and appreciation burns in their eyes.

"Ready?" Damien walks in front of me and I follow his broad back. He's always been an asshole, but since we married two weeks ago, he's moved so high on the asshole scale that I barely recognize him.

Once I step out of the hotel, I push a pair of large black glasses up on my face. Damien holds the door open, his fingers dance over his phone. His attention solely on his phone and not on me. I climb in with a sense of dis-satisfaction at how this all turned out. I had planned to storm his office and demand for him to take me shopping, only I had expected some kind of reaction. The car dips as he gets in and places his phone in its dock.

"Seatbelt." His one-word sentences have me clipping the belt in with a loud click. If he notices, he doesn't show it as he pulls out onto the main road.

Damien's fingers dance across the phone again until the ring fills the car. I glare out the window, but I'm aware of everything about Damien: his cologne; the space he takes up; the space that's empty between us. Yeah, I hate how aware of him I am.

"Terry, get Andrew on the phone and tell him to get to work. If he doesn't, he's not welcome back."

"Yes, sir." Terry's shaky voice has me glancing at Damien.

He ends the call and glares at me.

"I like Andrew, you won't fire him." I give the command and smile at my husband.

He sneers but the heavy breath holds no humor. "I don't have time today, Maria, so be quick."

Silly, silly Damien. Now I'll make sure I take my sweet time.

We pull into a space near the front of the mall. Damien busies himself with his phone, his fingers moving across the screen again as he removes the keys from the ignition and climbs out.

I unbuckle my belt and get out, fixing my short skirt. I didn't even want to shop. Closing the door, the car bleeps. Damien's talking on the phone, rambling off our location.

A group of young people hang out to the left of the door. They must be in their early twenties. One of the guys with a backwards cap wolf-whistles at me. I give him a smile. I appear older than them in my outfit and high heels.

The whistles cease abruptly and I glance back at the group who all look away. Frowning, I peek at Damien who's on his phone again.

My destination has pink neon signs outside. My lips tug up. If this doesn't get a reaction, I'm all out of ideas.

I pick up my pace and Damien matches it. When I peek at him he's looking around him. Not at me. Never at me.

Entering the store, the dim lights make it a very intimate setting.

"Good morning." I'm greeted when I step in and take off my sunglasses.

"Morning." I sing back in my chirpiest voice. The assistant's eyes jump to the looming figure behind me. Her eyes flash with appreciation. I want to tell her he might look like a rising God—or Devil—but he has a personality that could freeze Hell over. Yep, that cold.

I don't think, but randomly select lingerie. My fingers run across the red lacy material as I check the size.

"Can I help you?" The same blonde assistant who greeted us appears.

"That would be fantastic. It's my boyfriend's birthday and I want to wow him."

The blonde's eyes widen. I gaze at her name tag. Elaine.

"Red is his favorite color," I say holding up the red lacy bra.

Elaine gets to work, selecting a red thong, stockings and a black and red suspender belt.

"You can try them on."

My lips tug up higher. "That would be so great." I turn to Damien who looks like he's watching paint dry.

Smiling at Elaine, I take all the goods and follow her to the fitting rooms.

"Oh, I'm sorry sir, you can't be back here." Something in me sings. He followed me, that's what I wanted.

"I'll be right outside." I think his words are for me, but it's hard to tell as he walks out of the fitting room.

"Is he the boyfriend?" Elaine asks as I start to strip.

"No, that's my husband." I push down the skirt with frustration.

"Oh." Elaine's eyebrows rise into her hairline, before she composes herself and draws the curtain around me. Once the world is blocked off I slump down onto the chair. I refuse to meet my eyes in the mirror.

Irritation has me getting into the outfit. I have to get Elaine in to help me clip on the suspender belt. The end result...I would expect to cause a few heads to turn, but there's only one in particular I want to turn. I push back the curtain and move back dangerously close to the opening that leads out onto the floor. From the corner of my eye, his bulking form is there.

"What do you think?" I ask while checking out the back in the mirror. My heart pounds a little faster. I glance at Damien and his eyes skitter across my skin. Goosebumps rise in the wake of his stare.

"It's nice." He turns away with his phone.

Nice? I glance back at myself in the mirror. Nice? I know sexy and this screams sex. Not that I've ever had sex before. My father and brother make sure of that with their overprotective nature.

I pull the curtain around me with more force than necessary and get dressed. I move past Damien quickly as I go to the till and Elaine rings up my purchases. Her eyes keep jumping to Damien. I snort and her cheeks grow red as she focuses on her job. I want to tell her not to bother. He's made of stone. She smiles at him, and when I glance at him, his lip tugs up slightly at her.

Taking my purchases and card from a very distracted assistant, I slap on my glasses and walk as fast as I can in my heels. Damien manages to move beside me like I'm not speed walking in heels. His phone rings and he answers the device that consumes nearly all his attention. Maybe he should have married his phone.

I exhale as the car bleeps and I climb in. I could demand to go somewhere else. Does it matter? Two weeks of this bullshit and yet he avoids me like he got a raw deal.

When my father told me if I didn't marry Damien I wouldn't get my inheritance, I honestly wasn't that outraged. Arranged marriage isn't my thing, but Damien has always caught my attention—and I had thought I'd shown up on his radar a few times.

"I have to get back to the office. I'll drop you off at the house. Nate will be there."

I stare out the window and don't answer Damien. He doesn't seem to care as he drives me back to my gilded cage. My stomach twists and a scream pushes its way up my throat. I squash it as the gates open and we roam up the winding driveway to our marital home. Gifted by my father. The car stops at the main door and Nate appears. The engine still hums.

I glance at Damien and he's watching me. Green eyes consume me and I'm drowning. How easily he can strip me with one glance.

"I have to go, Maria."

I blink and he looks away. Grabbing my shopping bag, I get out of the car. The door clicks behind me and the car tears down the driveway.

"Hello, Princess." Nate greets me.

I take off my sunglasses.

"What's with the long face?"

I'll never tell anyone about how I feel. "Nothing, just Damien pissing me off as usual," I say as we enter the house. Kicking off my heels, I leave them, and my shopping bag, on the floor.

"Could you not find a top in your size?" I tease. Nate's white muscle top is painted onto his hard chest like a second skin.

"I'm your eye candy. I do this for you."

I grin at him. "I'm more of a suit kind of girl." I'm more of a Damien kind of girl.

Everyone in this house knows our marriage was arranged. At first it didn't bother me. But with each dismissal it becomes more painful to be rejected by him.

"You want a drink?" Nate calls as I take the steps up the stairs two at a time.

"Yeah, a Diet Coke." I call over the banister and climb to the first floor. Opening the doors to the master bedroom, I don't look at the unused bed. Flicking on the light, the closet space is illuminated. I shimmy into the black jeans before pulling on a hoodie. Today is a write-off. Swiping my hair up into a bun, I make my way back downstairs.

Nate smiles at me as I enter the kitchen. The tiles are cold under my bare feet. The can is colder as I wrap my fingers around it.

"I see you were shopping." Nate raises an eyebrow.

I shrug. "Yeah, I needed some stuff."

He could look in the bag and call me out on my lie, but Nate doesn't. Instead, he follows me into the living area. I fall back onto the couch and Nate joins me. I'm very aware of how close he sits and how our thighs touch. I can flirt and tease men, but having contact with them, I haven't experienced before. My brain misfires signals telling me Nate's closeness is calculated.

"I would have taken you shopping." I glance at him. His soft brown eyes travel across my face.

I frown. "It's fine, my husband did." I take a sip and allow my words to sink in. Nate still smiles and I know my brain has definitely misfired the signals to me.

"Aren't you sick of babysitting me?" I lean back on the couch and stare at the ceiling.

"No."

Men and their one-word answers. I get off the couch.

"Where are you going?"

"Where can I go?" I fire back.

"Wherever you want, Maria."

I glance at Nate and frown again. "No, I can't." He knew I couldn't go anywhere without someone watching over me. I knew my life before Damien had been overseen by my father, and that had been suffocating. With Damien, it felt worse. He was never here, yet someone else always was. At least with my father, I had him or my brother.

"Where do you want to go?" Nate asks.

"Rome." I fire out randomly. I don't want to see Rome, but I also want to drive my point home.

"Let me see what I can do." Nate's confidence has me laughing as I climb the stairs.

Not a chance.

Download and read HERE: https://author-vicarter.com/products/dark

Or scan the code below:

OTHER BOOKS BY VI CARTER

THE CELLS OF KALASHOV

THE COLLECTOR #1

THE SIXTH #2

THE HANDLER #3

MURPHY'S MAFIA MADE MEN

SINNER'S VOW #1

SAVAGE MARRIAGE #2

SCANDALOUS PLEDGE #3

SONS OF THE MAFIA

SINS OF THE MAFIA #0.5

VENGEANCE IN BLOOD #1

YOUNG IRISH REBELS SERIES

MAFIA PRINCE #1

MAFIA KING #2

MAFIA GAMES #3

MAFIA BOSS #4

MAFIA SECRETS #5 (NOVELLA)

WILD IRISH SERIES

FATHER (PREQUEL)

VICIOUS #1

RECKLESS #2

RUTHLESS #3

FEARLESS #4

HEARTLESS #5

<u>THE BOYNE CLUB</u>

DARK #1

DARKER # 2

DARKEST #3

PITCH BLACK #4

<u>THE OBSESSED DUET</u>

A DEADLY OBSESSION #1

A CRUEL CONFESSION #2

<u>BROKEN PEOPLE DUET</u>

BREAK ME #1

SAVE ME #2

ABOUT THE AUTHOR

V i Carter - the queen of **DARK ROMANCE**, the mistress of suspense, and the high priestess of *PLOT TWISTS*!

When she's not busy crafting tales of the **MAFIA** that'll leave you on the edge of your seat, you can find her baking up a storm, exploring the gorgeous Irish countryside, or spending time with her three little girls.

Vi's Young Irish Rebels series has been praised by readers and can be found in English, Dutch, German, Audible and soon will be available in French.

And let's not forget her two greatest loves: ***coffee and chocolate***. If you ever need to bribe her, just offer up a mug of coffee and a slab of chocolate, and she'll be putty in your hands.

So, if you're ready to join Vi on a wild journey with the mafia, sign up for her newsletter and score a free book! Just be warned - her stories are so **ADDICTIVE**, you might not be able to put them down.

Editorial Reviews

"Vi Carter has once again blown my mind with another outstanding story. She never fails to create a masterpiece with memorable characters that leap off the page. This book is complete perfection."- USA Today Bestselling Author Khardine Gray

Vi is one of those authors who never disappoints. She weaves **LOVE** & **DANGER** effortlessly. ★★★★★ stars

I definitely recommend this book. It is **SUSPENSEFUL** and exciting. I enjoy reading Vi Carter's book. ★★★★★ stars

How to Keep in Touch with Vi Carter

Visit Vi's website: https://author-vicarter.com/

Join the newsletter: t.ly/yZWbX

Or scan the code below:

DARK

On Facebook, Instagram, TikTok and YouTube @darkauthorvicarter and
on Twitter @authorvicarter
Or scan the code below: